Brian Wilson Aldiss was born in Norfolk in 1925. He wrote his first novel, *The Brightfount Diaries* (1955), while working as a bookseller in Oxford. But he is perhaps better known as one of the most noteworthy voices in science fiction writing. His first work of science fiction, *Non-Stop*, appeared in 1958. Since then, he has written over 40 novels and 300 short stories, as well as poetry and critical works, and received all of the major science fiction awards. He has reviewed for the *Times Literary Supplement*, the *Guardian* and the *Washington Post*, and he has edited *Science Fiction Horizons*, as well as several anthologies. Brian Aldiss recently celebrated his seventy-fifth birthday and is presently working on several new books.

CRYPTOZOIC!

Brian Aldiss

HOUSE OF
STRATUS

This edition published in 2000 by House of Stratus, an imprint of
Stratus Holdings plc, 24c Old Burlington Street, London, W1X 1RL, UK.

www.houseofstratus.com

Typeset, printed and bound by House of Stratus.

A catalogue record for this book is available from the British Library.

ISBN 0-7551-0053-0

*For James Blish whose cities
fly words too*

CONTENTS

BOOK ONE

BOOK TWO

In te, anime meus, tempora metior.
ST. AUGUSTINE: Confessions, Bk. II

"It's a poor sort of memory that only works
backwards," the Queen remarked.
LEWIS CARROLL: *Through the Looking Glass*

They lay heaped about meaninglessly, and yet with a terrible meaning that hinted of the force which had flung them here. They seemed to be something between the inorganic and the organic. They proliferated on the margins of time, embodying all the amazing forms the world was to carry; the earth was having a nightmare of stone about the progeny that would swarm over it.

These copromorphic forms suggested, elephants, seals, diplodoci, strange squamata and sauropods, beetles, bats, octopoidal fragments, penguins, woodlice, hippos, living or dying.

Ungainly reminders of the human physique also appeared: torsos, thighs, groins lightly hollowed, backbones, breasts, suggestion of hands and fingers, massive shoulders, phallic shapes: all distinct and yet all merged with the stranger anatomies about them in this forlorn agony of nature – and all moulded mindlessly out of the grey putty without thought turned out, without thought to be obliterated.

They stretched as far as the eye could see, piled on top of each other, as if they filled the entire Cryptozoic...or as if they were the sinister fore-shadowings of what was to come as well as the after-images of what was long past...

BOOK ONE

chapter one

a bed in the old red sandstone

The sea level had been slowly sinking for the last few thousand years. It lay so nearly motionless that one could hardly tell whether its small waves broke from it against the shore or were in some way formed at the shoreline and cast back into the deep. The river disgorging into the sea had built up bars of red mud and shingle, thus often hindering its own way with gravel banks or casting off wide pools which stagnated in the sunshine. A man appeared to be sitting by one of these pools. Although he seemed to be surrounded by green growth, behind him the beach was as bare as a dried bone.

The man was tall and loose-limbed. He was fair-haired, pale-skinned, and his expression in repose held something morose and watchful in it. He wore a one-piece garment and carried a knapsack strapped to his back, in which were his pressurized water ration, food substitutes, some artist's materials and two notebooks. About his neck he wore a device popularly known as an air-leaker, which consisted of a loose-fitting hoop that had a small motor attachment at the back and in front, under the chin, a small nozzle that breathed fresh air into the man's face.

The man's name was Edward Bush. He was a solitary man some forty-five elapsed years old. As far as he could be said to be thinking at all, he was brooding about his mother.

At this phase of his life, he found himself becalmed, without direction. His temporary job for the Institute did nothing to alleviate this inward feeling that he had come to an uncharted crossroads. It was as though all his psychic mechanisms had petered out, or stood idling, undecided whether to venture this way or that under the force of some vast prodromic unease.

Resting his chin on his knee, Bush stared out over the dull expanse of sea. Somewhere, he could hear motorbikes revving.

He did not want anyone to see what he was doing. He jumped up and hurried across to his easel. He had walked away from it in disgust; it was farther away than he remembered. The painting was no damned good, of course; he was finished as an artist. Maybe that was why he could not face going back to the present.

Howells would be waiting for his report at the Institute. Bush had drawn Howells into the picture. He had tried to express emptiness, staring out at the sea, working with flooded paper and aquarelles – in mind-travel, such primitive equipment was all one could manage to carry.

The heavy colour came flooding off the ends of the pencils. Bush had gone berserk. Over the sullen sea, a red-faced sun with Howells' features had risen.

He began to laugh. A stunted tree to one side of the canvas: he applied the pencil to it.

"Mother-figure!" he said. "It's you, Mother! Just to show I haven't forgotten you."

His mother's features stared out of the foliage. He gave her a diamond crown; his father often called her Queen – half in love, half in irony. So his father was in the picture too, suffusing it.

Bush stood looking down at the canvas.

"It's masterly, you know!" he said to the shadowy woman who stood behind him, some distance away, not regarding him. He seized up an aquarelle and scrawled a title to it: FAMILY GROUP. After all, he was in it too. It was all him.

4

Then he pulled the paper block from the clamp, tore off the daub, and screwed it up.

He folded the easel small and stuck it into his pack.

The sun shone behind Bush, over low hills, preparing to set. The hills were bare except along the riverbed, where runty little leafless psilophyton grew in the shade of primitive lycopods. Bush cast no shadow.

The distant sound of motorbikes, the only sound in the great Devonian silence, made him nervous. At the fringe of his vision, a movement on the ground made him jump. Four lobe fins jostled in a shallow pool, thrashing into the shallows. They struggled over the red mud, their curiously armoured heads lifted off the ground as they peered ahead with comic eagerness. Bush made as if to photograph them with his wrist camera, and then thought better of it; he had photographed lobe fins before.

The legged fish snapped at insects crawling on the mud banks or nosed eagerly in rotting vegetation. In the days of his genius, he had used an abstraction of their viridian armoured heads for one of his most successful works.

The noise of the bikes ceased. He scrutinized the landscape, climbing on to a bank of shingle to get a better view; there might or might not be a cluster of people far down the beach. The ocean was almost still. The phantom dark-haired woman was still. In one sense, she was company; in another, she was just one of the irritating ghosts of his overburdened brains.

"It's like a bloody textbook!" he called to her mockingly. "This beach... Evolution... Lack of oxygen in the dying sea... Fish getting out. Their adventure into space... And of course my father would read religion into it all." Cheered by the sound of his own voice, he began to recite (his father was a great quoter of poetry): "Spring... Too long... Gongula..." Too bloody long.

Ah well, you had to have your fun, or you'd go mad here. He breathed in air through the air-leaker, looking askance at his custodian. The dark-haired woman was still there, dim and insubstantial as always. She was doing some sort of guard duty he decided. He held out a hand to her, but could no more touch her than he could the lobe fins or the red sand.

Lust, that was his trouble. He needed this isolation while his inward clocks stood still, but was also bored by it. Lust would get him stirring again; yet the Dark Woman was as unattainable as the improper women of his imagination.

It was no pleasure to him to see the bare hills through her body. He lay down on the gravel, his body resting more or less on the configurations of its slope. Rather than wrestle with the problem of her identity, he turned back to the moody sea, staring at it as if he hoped to see some insatiable monster break from the surface and shatter the quiescence with which he was inundated.

All beaches were connected. Time was nothing to beaches. This one led straight to the beach he had known one miserable childhood holiday, when his parents quarrelled with suppressed violence, and he had trembled behind a hut with grit in his shoes, eavesdropping on their hatred. If only he could forget his childhood, he could begin creative life anew! Perhaps an arrangement of hut-like objects... Enshrined by time...

Characteristic of him that he should lie here meditating his next spatial-kinetic groupage, rather than actually tackling it; but his art (ha!) had brought him easy rewards too early – more because he was one of the first artists to mind-travel, he suspected, than because the public was particularly struck by his solitary genius, or by his austere and increasingly monochromatic arrangements of movable blocks and traps expressing those obscure spatial relationships and time synchronizations which for Bush constituted the world.

In any case, he was finished with the purely photic-signal-type groupages that had brought him such success five years ago. Instead of dragging that load of externals inward, he would push the internals outward, related to macro-cosmic time. He would if he knew how to begin.

Bush could hear the motorbikes again, thudding along the deserted beach. He pushed them away, indulging further his train of thought, his head full of angles and leverages that would not resolve into anything that could move him to expression. He had plunged into mind-travel at the Institute's encouragement, deliberately to disrupt his circadian rhythms, so that he could grapple with the new and fundamental problems of time perception with which his age was confronted – and had found nothing that would resolve into expression. Hence his dereliction on this shore.

Old Claude Monet had pursued the right sort of path, considering his period, sitting there patiently at Giverny, transforming water lilies and pools into formations of colour that conspired towards an elusive statement on time. Monet had never been saddled with the Devonian, or the Palaeozoic Era.

The human consciousness had now widened so alarmingly, was so busy transforming everything on Earth into its own peculiar tones, that no art could exist that did not take proper cognisance of the fact. Something entirely new had to be forged; even the bio-electro-kinetic sculpture of the previous decade was old hat.

He had the seeds of that new art in his life, which, as he had long ago recognized, followed the scheme of a vortex, his emotions pouring down into a warped centre of being, always on the move, pressing forward like a storm, but always coming back to the same point. The painter who stirred him most was old Joseph Mallord William Turner; his life, set in another period when technology was altering ideas of time, had also moved in vortices, just as his later canvases had been dominated by that pattern.

The vortex: symbol of the way every phenomenon in the universe swirled round into the human eye, like water out of a basin.

So he had thought a thousand times. The thought also whirled round and round, getting nowhere.

Grunting to himself, Bush sat up to look for the motorbikes.

They were about half a mile away, stationary on the dull beach; he could see them clearly; objects in his own dimension showed much darker than they would have done if they existed in the world outside, the entropy barrier cutting down about ten per cent of the light. The ten riders showed up rather like cut-outs against the exotic Devonian backdrop, all forces conspiring to admit that they did not and never would belong here.

The bikes were the light models their riders could carry back in mind-travel with them. They spun round in intricate movements, throwing up no sand where one might expect parabolas of it, splashing no wave when they appeared to drive through the waves. That which they had never affected, they had no power to affect now. As miraculously, they managed to avoid each other, finally coming to rest in a neat straight line, some facing one way, some the other, their horizontal discs hovering just above the sand.

Bush watched as the riders climbed off and set about inflating a tent. All of them wore the green buckskin which was virtually the uniform of their kind. One he saw, had long streaming yellow hair – a woman perhaps. Although he could not tell from this distance, his interest was aroused.

After a while, the riders spotted him sitting on the red gravel and four of them began to walk towards him. Bush felt self-conscious, but remained where he was, at first pretending he had not seen them.

They were tall. All wore high peel-down buckskin boots. They carried their air-leakers carelessly slung round their necks. One had a reptile skull painted on his helmet. As usual with such groups, they were all between thirty and forty – hence their other nickname, "Tershers" – since that was the youngest age group that could afford to hit mind-travel. One of them was a girl.

Although Bush was nervous to see them marching up, he felt an immediate attack of lust at the sight of the girl. She was the one with the long yellow hair. It looked untended and greasy, and her face was utterly without make-up. Her features were sharp but at the same time indeterminate, her gaze somewhat unfocused. Her figure was slight. It might be her damned boots, he jeered to himself, for she was not immediately attractive, but the feeling persisted.

"What are you doing here, chum?" one of the men asked, staring down at Bush.

Bush thought it was time he stood up, remaining where he was only because to stand up might look threatening.

"Resting, till you lot roared up." He looked over the man who had spoken. A blunt-nosed fellow with deep creases under each cheek that nobody would dare or want to call dimples; nothing to recommend him: scrawny, scruffy, highly strung.

"You tired or something?"

Bush laughed; the pretence of concern in the tersher's voice was pitched exactly right. Tension left him and he replied, "You could say that – cosmically tired, at a standstill. See these armoured fish here?" He put his foot through where the lobe fins appeared to be, gobbling in the sea-wrack. "I've been lying here all day watching them evolve."

The tershers laughed. One of them said, cheekily, "We thought you was lying there trying to evolve yourself. Look as if you could do with it!"

Evidently he had appointed himself group humorist and was not much appreciated. The others ignored him and the leader said, "You're mad! You'll get swept away by the tide, you will!"

"It's been going out for the last million years. Don't you read the newspapers?" As they laughed at that, he climbed to his feet and dusted himself down – purely instinctively, for he had never touched the sand.

They were in contact now. Looking at the leader, Bush said, "Got anything to eat you'd care to swap for food tablets?"

The girl spoke for the first time. "A pity we can't grab some of your evolving fish and cook them. I still can't get used to that sort of thing – the isolation."

She had sound teeth, though they probably needed as good a scrub as the rest of her.

"Been here long?" he said.

"Only left 2090 last week."

He nodded. "I've been here two years. At least, I haven't been back to – the present for two years, two and a half years. Funny to think that by our time these walking fish will be asleep in the Old Red Sandstone!"

'We're making our way up to the Jurassic," the leader said, elbowing the girl out of the way. "Been there?"

"Sure, I hear it's getting more like a fairground every year."

"We'll find ourselves a place if we have to clear one."

"There's forty-six million years of it," Bush said, shrugging.

He walked with them back to the rest of the group, who stood motionless among the inflated tents.

"I'd like to involve into one of them big Jurassic animals, with big teeth," the humorist said. "Tyrannosaurs or whatever they call 'em. I'd be as tough as you then, Lenny!"

Lenny was the leader with the excoriated dimples. The funny one was called Pete. The girl's name was Ann; she belonged to Lenny. None of the group used names much, except Pete. Bush said his name was Bush, and left it like that. There were six men, each with a bike, and four girls who had evidently blasted into the Devonian on the back of the men's bikes. None of the girls was attractive, except for Ann. They all settled by the bikes, lounging or standing; Bush was the only one who sat. He looked cautiously round for the Dark Woman; she had disappeared; just as well – remote though she was, she might sense more clearly than anyone else here the reason why Bush had tagged along with the gang.

The only other person in the group whom Bush marked out as interesting was an older man obviously not a tersher at all, although he wore the buckskin. His hair was a dead black, probably dyed, and under his long nose his mouth had settled into a wry expression that seemed worth a moment's curiosity.

He said nothing, though his searching glance at Bush spoke of an alert mind.

"Two years you been minding, you say?" Lenny said. "You a millionaire or something?"

"Painter. Artist Grouper. I do spatial-kinetic groupages, SKGs, if you know what they are. And I can operate back here for Wenlock Institute. How do you all afford to get here?"

Lenny scorned to answer the question. He said, challengingly, "You're lying, mate! You never work for the Institute! Look – I ain't a fool! – I know they only send recorders out into the past for eighteen months at a time at the most. Two and a half years: what are you on about? You can't kid me!"

"I wouldn't bother to kid you! I *do* work for the Institute. It's true I came back for an eighteen-month term, but I've – I've overstayed for an extra year, that's all."

Lenny glared at him in contempt. "They'll have your guts for garters!"

"They won't! If you must know, I'm one of their star minders. I can get nearer the present than anyone else on their books."

"You aren't very near now, lounging about in the Devonian! Not that I believe your story anyway."

"Believe or not, as you please," Bush said. He loathed cross-questioning and shook with anger as Lenny turned away.

Unmoved by the argument, one of the other tershers said, 'We had to work, get cash, take the CSD shot, come back here. Lot of money. Lot of work! Still don't believe we're really here."

"We aren't. The universe is, but we aren't. Or rather, the universe may be and we aren't. They still aren't sure which way it is. There's a lot about mind-travel that still has to be understood." He was heavy and patronizing to cover his disturbance.

"Would you paint us?" Ann asked him. It was the only reaction he got to his announcement that he was a painter.

*

He looked her in the eye. He thought he understood the glance that passed involuntarily between them. One gratifying thing about growing older was that you misinterpreted such looks more rarely.

"If you interested me I would."

"Only we don't want to be painted, see," Lenny said.

"I wasn't volunteering to do it. What sort of work did you do to earn the cash to get here?"

Bush was not interested in their answer. He was looking at Ann, who had dropped her gaze. He thought that he could feel her – nothing could be touched in the limbo of mind-travel, but she was from his time, so she would respond to touch.

One of the anonymous tershers answered him. "Except for Ann here, and Josie, we all ganged on the new Bristol mind-station. We was some of the first to mind through when it was finished. Know it?"

"I designed the SKG, the groupage in the foyer – the synchronized-signal nodal re-entry symbol with the powered interlocking vanes. 'Progression', it's called."

"That bloody thing!" As he spoke, Lenny pulled the cigarlet from his mouth and sent it spinning toward the slow motion sea. The end lay just above the waves, glowing, until lack of oxygen extinguished it.

"Me, I liked it," Pete said. "Looked like a couple of record-breaking watches had run into each other on a dark night and were signalling for help!" He laughed vacuously.

"You shouldn't laugh at yourself. You just gave us a pretty good description of all this." Bush swung his hand about to take in the visible and invisible universe.

"Piss off!" Lenny said, heaving himself from his bike and moving over to Bush. "You are so smart and boring, Jack! You can just piss off!"

Bush got up. But for the girl, he would have pissed off. He had no inclination to be beaten up by this mob. "If you don't care for my conversation, why don't *you* supply some?"

"You talk rubbish, that's why. That business about the Old Red Sandstone…"

"It's true! You may not like it, or care about it, but it's not rubbish." He pointed at the older man with dark dyed hair, standing slightly apart from the group. "Ask him! Ask your girlfriend. Up in 2090, all that you see here is compressed into a few feet of rumpled red rock – shingle, fish, plants, sunlight, moonlight, the very breeze, all solidified down into something the geologists hack out of the earth with pickaxes. If you don't know about that or you aren't moved by the poetry of it, why bother to blue ten years' savings to come back here?"

"I'm not saying nothing about that, chum, I'm saying you bore me."

"It's entirely mutual." He had gone as far as he was prepared to go, and it seemed that Lenny had too, for he backed away indifferently when Ann came in and shouted them both down.

"He *talks* like an artist, doesn't he?" the plump little Josie said, mainly addressing the older man. "I think there's something in what he says. We aren't getting the best out of it here, really, I mean. It is a bit marvellous here, isn't it, long before there were any men or women on the globe?"

"The capacity for wonder is available to everyone. But most people are afraid of it." The older man had spoken.

Lenny gave a bark of contempt. "Don't you start in, Stein!"

"I mean, there's the sea where it all started, and here we are. We can't touch it, of course." Josie was wrestling with concepts too awful and vague for her mental equipment, judging by the tranced look on her face. "Funny, I look at this sea and I can't help thinking we're at the *end* of the world, not the beginning."

This chimed strangely with something Bush had been meditating on earlier in the day; the girl had a beautiful idea, and for an instant he debated switching his attentions to her. The others looked glum; it was their way of registering profundity. Lenny slung himself on to his bike and kicked the starter, and the two air columns began to blow at once. It still looked like a defiance of a physical law that the sand lay under them undisturbed; and so it was. All round them was the invisible but unyielding wall of mind-travel. The four other tersher boys climbed on to their bikes, two of the girls jumping up behind. They snarled away down the darkening sand. Dark was coming, the low bristles of vegetation stirred with an onshore breeze; but in the mind dimension, all was still. Bush was left standing with the older man, Josie, and Ann.

"So much for supper," he commented. "If I'm not wanted, I'll be off. I have a camp just up in the first series of hills." He gestured towards the sunset, looking all the while at Ann.

"You mustn't mind Lenny," Ann said. "He's moody." She looked at him. She really had next to no figure, he told himself, and she was dirty and scruffy; it did not stop him trembling. The isolation of mind-travel could bring on complete dissociation of character; once in it, one could feel nothing, smell nothing, hear nothing, except one's fellow travellers. This girl – she was like the prospect of a banquet! And there was more to it than that – *what* he could not yet determine.

"Now that those who do not wish to discuss vital subjects are away, you can sit and talk with us," said the older man. It could have been that wry expression, or maybe he was in some way mocking.

"I've overstayed my welcome. I'm off!"

To his surprise, the older man came and shook his hand.

"You keep strangest company," Bush said. He was not interested in this fellow, whoever he was.

He started back along the beach towards his own lonely camp, the uselessness of playing about with Lenny's girl uppermost in his mind. The dark thing out to sea had spread monstrous wings and was in flight for the land. He suddenly felt the utter senselessness of setting down Man in such a gigantic universe and then letting him challenge it – or of giving him desires he could neither control or fulfil.

14

Ann said, "I can't get used to the way we can't touch anything of the real world. It really bugs me. I – you know, I don't feel I exist."

She was walking beside him. He could hear the sound of her boots slapping against her legs.

"I've adapted. It's the smell of the place I miss. The air-leakers don't give you a whisper of what it smells like."

"Life never gives you enough."

He stopped. "Must you follow me? You're going to get me into trouble. Beat it back to your lover boy – you can see I'm not your kind."

"We haven't proved it yet."

Momentarily, they looked desperately at each other, as if some enormous thing had to be resolved in silence.

They trudged on. Bush had made up his mind now; or rather, he had no mind. It had gone from him, sunk under the ocean of his bloodstream, in the tides of which it seemed to him that direction was being born anew. They scrambled together into the river valley, hurrying upstream along the bank, clasping each other's hands. Only momentarily was he aware of what he was doing.

"What's got into you?"

"You're crazy!"

"You're crazy!"

They hurried over a bed of large and broken shells. He could have cut his hand on one. He'd looked them up in the guide book earlier. Phragmoceras. At first he had thought they were some animal's teeth, not the deserted home of an early cephalopod. Silurian, maybe, sharpened by the sea to draw his quaternary blood, had not mind-travel built that impenetrable barrier between what-had-been and what-was. The shells did not even crunch as he and the girl climbed over them. Glancing down in his fever, he saw their feet were under the level of the shells, treading on the spongy floor that belonged to their dimension rather than the Devonian period – a sort of lowest common denominator of floors.

They stopped in a sheltered dell. They clung to each other. Eagerly, they glared into each other's faces in the waning light. He could not remember how long they stood like that, or what they said – except for one remark of hers: "We're millions of years from our birth – we ought to be free to do it, oughtn't we?"

What had he answered – anything she might find valuable? Anything he could give? He recalled only how he had thrown her down, pulled off her swashbuckling boots, helped her drag off her trousers, torn his own away from him. She behaved as if she had been switched on to overdrive, was immediately absolutely and irresistibly ready for him, seized him strongly.

He recalled after, obsessively over and over, the particular gesture with which she had raised one bent leg to admit him to her embrace, and his surprise and his gratitude to find that up and down the howling gulf of centuries there was this sweet hole to go to.

While they were resting, they heard the motorbikes roaring like distant thwarted animals. It merely roused them to a repetition of love.

"You smell so damned sweet! You're beautiful!" His words reminded him of how dressed they still were, so that he pushed her shirt and tunic up in order to kiss her nipples.

"We should be as naked as savages… We are savages, aren't we, Bush?"

"Thank God, yes. You've no idea how far from the savage I am usually. Mother-dominated, full of doubts and fears. Not like your Lenny!"

"Him? He's a nut case! He's scared really – scared of all this…"

"Of loving, you mean? Or of the space-time world?"

"That, yes. He's scared of everything underneath. His old man used to beat him up."

Their faces were close together. They were fainter than the dusk gathering about them, sinking forever into the complexities of their own minds.

"I'm afraid of him. Or I was when you lot first appeared. I thought they'd beat me up! It's all very well – what's the matter, Ann?"

She sat up and began to pull her tunic down. "Got a fag? I didn't come here to hear how chicken you were. Bugger all that! You men are all the same – all got something wrong with you!"

"We're not all the same, not by a long chalk! But now's a time to talk. I haven't talked intimately to anyone for months. I've been locked up in silence. And nothing to touch... You get pursued by phantoms. I really ought to get back to 2090 to see my mother, but I'll be in trouble when I turn up... It's so long since I screwed a girl...honest, I began to imagine I was going queer or something."

"What makes you say that?" she asked tartly.

"The desire to be honest while I can. That's a luxury, isn't it?"

"Well, lay off, if you don't mind! I don't go slobbering all over you, do I, with a lot of nonsense? I didn't come with you for that."

A moment before, Bush had felt nothing but love for her. Now he was overwhelmed by anger. He flung her garments at her.

"Put your pants on and hop off back to your yobbo boyfriend if you feel like that about it! Why did you follow me in the first place?"

She put a hand on his arm, immune from his anger. "I made a mistake. I thought you might be a bit different." She blew smoke at him. "Don't worry, I enjoyed the mistake. You're quite good at it, even if you are queer!"

He jumped up, pulling on his trousers without dignity, raging – against himself more than against Ann. He turned, and Lenny was outlined against the lemon sky. Mastering himself, he zipped himself up and stood his ground.

Lenny had also stopped. He turned his head and called to the other tershers. "He's up here!"

"Come and get me if you want me!" Bush said. He was frightened; if they broke his fingers he might never be able to work properly again. Or blinded him. There weren't any police patrols here; they could do what they liked with him; they had all the wide Devonian to bash him up in. Then he recalled what Ann had said; Lenny was scared too.

He went slowly forward, Lenny had a tool of some kind, a spanner, in his hand. "I'm going to get you, Bush!" he said, glancing over his shoulders to see that the others were supporting him. Bush jumped on him, got his arms round him, swung him savagely. The tersher was unexpectedly light. He staggered as Bush let him go. As he brought up the spanner, Bush hit him in the face, then stepped back as if to leave it at that.

"Hit him again!" Ann called.

He hit Lenny again, Lenny kicked him on the kneecap. He fell, grabbed Lenny's legs and pulled him down too. Lenny raised the spanner again, Bush grabbed his wrist, and they rolled over, struggling. At last Bush got his knee in the other's crutch, and the tersher gave up the fight. Panting, Bush got to his feet, clasping his kneecap. The other four boys of the gang were lined up near him.

"Who's next?" he asked. When they showed no inclination to move, he pointed to their leader. "Get him up! Get him out of here!"

Feebly, they moved to obey. One of them said sullenly, "You're just a bully. We didn't do you no harm. Ann's Lenny's girl."

The wish to fight left him. From their point of view, they were perfectly correct in looking at it that way. True, their manner from the start had offended him, but possibly they were less responsible for that than he had allowed.

"I'm off," he announced. "Lenny can keep his girl!"

It was time to mind again. He'd get to a safe place and then he would mind to another time and space. He picked his way into the hills, looking back frequently to see they were not following him. After a while, he heard their motorbikes, was aware of the loneliness of the sound, turned to watch their lasered lights vanish down the strand. The Dark Woman was phantasmally there; he watched the disappearing lights through her form. He had no doubt that she was on duty, and that she came from some remote future of her own. Through the sockets of her eyes, the stars of Bootes glistened.

There was a noise near at hand, indicating someone in his own continuum, sandwiched with him between all the rest of time. The girl was following him.

'Wouldn't your yobbo boyfriend have you back?"

"Don't be like that, Bush! I want to talk to you."

"O God!" He took her arm, pulled her through the darkness. At least there were no obstacles to trip over on a generalized floor. Without saying a word more to each other, they climbed up to his tent and crawled in.

chapter two

up the entropy slope

When he woke, she was gone.

He lay for a long while looking up at the tent roof, wondering how much he cared. He needed company, although he was never wholly comfortable with it; he needed a woman, although he was never wholly happy with one. He wanted to talk, although he knew most talk was an admission of non-communication.

He washed and dressed and climbed outside. Of Ann there was no sign. But of course in mind nobody left any tracks behind, so that the vivid green vegetation on every side was untrampled, although Bush had walked through it a dozen times on his way to doing sentry duty with the lobe fins.

The sun shone. Its great untiring furnace poured down its warmth on a world in which the coal deposits had yet to be laid, in memory of a vintage period of its combustion. Bush had a headache.

For a while, he stood there scratching himself, wondering what had caused it: the excitements of the day before, or the relentless pressure of the empty eons. He decided it was the latter. Nobody could be said really to live in these vacant centuries; he and the tershers and the rest travelled back here, but their relationship to the actual Devonian was merely tentative. Man had conquered passing time; at least, the intellects at the Wenlock Institute had — but since passing time was no more than a tic (tick?) of homo sapiens, the universe remained unmoved by the accomplishment.

"Are you going to do a groupage of me?"

Bush turned. The girl was standing above him, some feet away. Because the dimension changed between them and the world filtered out light, she appeared dark and wraith-like. He could hardly see her face; mind-travel had reduced them all to spectres, even to each other.

"I thought you'd gone back to your friends!"

Ann came down to him. She was swinging her air-leaker carelessly. With her tunic open and her hair uncombed, she looked more of a vagabond than ever. Feeling his biceps, she said. "Did you *hope* I'd gone back or *fear* I'd gone back?"

He frowned at her, trying to make out what she was really like. Human relationships exhausted him; perhaps that was why he had hung about here so long, back in the vacuum of exhausted time.

"I can't make you out, girl. No offence. It's like looking through two thicknesses of glass. Nobody ever turns out to be what they seem."

She dropped her sharp look and scrutinized him almost sympathetically. "What's bugging you, sweetie? Something deep, isn't it?"

Her sympathy seemed to open up a wound. "I couldn't begin to tell you. Things are so involved in my head. It's all a muddle."

"Tell, if it'll make you feel better. I've got all the Devonian in the world!"

He shook his head. "What your girlfriend Josie said yesterday. That this should be the end of the world rather than the beginning, I could only get myself disentangled if that would happen, if I could start my life again."

Ann laughed. "Back to the womb, eh?"

He realized he did not feel well. That would have to be reported to the Institute; you could lose your mind back in these damned silent mazes. He could not reply to Ann, or face up to

21

her revolting suggestion. Sighing heavily, he went over to his tent and pulled the cord to let it deflate. It collapsed in a series of shudders; he never cared to watch the process, but now some chattering thing inside him gave a commentary on it, likening it to a disappointed womb from which a lucky child has managed to escape.

Stoically, he folded up the tent and put it away. With the girl standing watching him, he drew out his rations and made his simple preparations for breakfast. Mind-travellers carried a basic food kit, frugal in the extreme but easy to deal with. He had replenished his stores several times from other minders who were surfacing – returning to their present – early because they could not stand the silences, and from a friend of his who ran a small store in the Jurassic.

As his pan of beef essence steamed, he raised his eyes until they met the girl's and spoke again to her.

"Care to join me before you clear off?"

"Since you ask me so graciously..." She sat down by him, sprawling with legs apart, smiling at him – grateful even for my miserable company, Bush thought.

"I didn't mean to upset you, Bush! You're as touchy as Stein."

"Who's Stein?"

"The old guy – the one with the gang. You know – dyed hair – you spoke to him. He shook your hand."

"Oh, yes, Stein! How did he fall in with you and Lenny?"

"He was going to be beaten up or something and Lenny and the boys saved him. He's terribly nervous. You know, when he first saw you, he said you might be a spy. He's from 2093 and he says things are bad there."

Bush had no wish to think about the twenty-nineties and the dreary world in which his parents lived. He said, "Lenny has his good side, then?"

She nodded, but was pursuing her own line of thought.

"Stein had me scared about mind-travel. Do you know, he said that Wenlock might be all wrong about mind-travel, and that we might not really be here at all, or something like that? He said there was something sinister about the Undermind, and nobody understood it yet, despite all the claims of the Wenlock Institute."

"Well, it's all new as yet. The Undermind was only first developed as a concept of 2073, and the first mind-travel wasn't till two years later, so there may be more to discover, although it's difficult to see what it might be. What does Stein know about it, anyway?"

"Maybe he was just sounding off, trying to impress me."

"Did you let him — I mean, did he lie with you?"

"Jealous?" She grinned challengingly.

"What do you want me to say?" They stared at each other. Through the dirty pane of her face, he saw life shine. He reached forward and kissed her.

She lifted the boiling beef essence off his tiny stove and said, "I think I've about had the Devonian Period. How about moving on to the Jurassic with me?"

"Aren't Lenny and Co going there?"

"So what? There's forty-six million years of it..."

"Touché. What do you want to do there? See the carnivores mate?"

She gave him a sly look. "We could watch 'em together."

Instantly, he was excited. He slid a hand across her buckskin thigh.

"I'll come with you." As they drank their essence, he was jeering at himself for getting mixed up with the girl; she was confused and could only upset his mental balance. It was true she was a good lay and not unintelligent, but he had never been satisfied to accept anyone else by compartments; her whole self did not seem accessible. And perhaps he was not the right person to help her render all of her personality accessible.

She snuggled against him. "I need someone to mind-travel with. I'd be frightened to let go on my own. My mother wouldn't mind-travel to save her life! People of that generation will never take to it, I suppose. Wow, 1 wish we could mind back just a little way – you know, one generation – because I'd so like to see my old man courting my mother and making love to her, I bet they made a proper muck-up of it, just as they did of anything else!"

When he said nothing, she nudged him. "Well, go on, say something! Wouldn't you like to see your parents at it? You aren't as stuffy as you make out, Bush, are you? You'd love it!"

"Ann, you just don't realize the horror of what you are saying!"

"Come on, you'd like it too!"

Bush shook his head. "I have enough data on my parents without the need for that sort of thing! But I suppose yours is the majority view. Dr Wenlock ran a questionnaire at the Institute about a decade ago – I mean in 2080 – which showed how strong incest-motivation is in mind-travellers. It's the force behind the predisposition to look back. The findings coincide with the old psycho-analytical view of human nature.

"Current theory suggests that man first became homo sapiens when he put a ban on – well, let's call it endogamy, the custom forbidding marriage outside the familial group. Exogamy was man's very first painful step forward. No other animal puts a ban on endogamy."

"Was it worth it!" Ann exclaimed.

"Well, since then man has become all the things we know he has become, conqueror of his environment and all that, but his severance from nature has seemed to grow wider and wider – I mean from his true nature.

"The way the Wenlockians see it, the undermind is, as it were, our old natural mind. The overmind is a later, homo sap accretion, a high-powered dynamo whose main function is to structure time and conceal all the sad animal thoughts in the undermind. The extremists claim that passing time is an invention of the overmind."

Perhaps she was not listening. She said. "You know why I followed you yesterday? I had the strongest feeling directly you appeared that you and I had – known each other terribly well at some past time."

"I'd have remembered you!"

"It must have been my undermind playing up! Anyhow, what you were saying was very interesting. I suppose you believe it, do you?"

He laughed. "How can you not believe it? We're in the Devonian, aren't we?"

"But if the undermind governs mind-travel, and the undermind's crazy about incest, then surely we should be able to visit times near at hand, early in our own century, for instance – so that we could see what our own parents and grandparents got up to. That would be *the* most interesting thing, wouldn't it? But it's much easier to mind back here, to the earliest ages of the world, and to get back to when there were any humans at all is very difficult. Impossible for most of us."

"That's so, but it doesn't prove what you think. If you think of the space-time universe as being an enormous entropy-slope, with the true present always at the point of highest energy and the farthest past at the lowest, then obviously as soon as our minds are free of passing time, they will fall backwards towards that lowest point, and the nearer to the highest point we return, the harder will be the journey."

Ann said nothing. Bush thought it likely that she had already dismissed the subject as impossible of discussion, but after a moment she said, "You know what you said about the real me being good and loving? Supposing there is such a person, is she in my over- or my undermind?"

"Supposing, as you say, there is such a person, she must be an amalgamation of both. Anything less than the whole cannot be whole."

"Now you're trying to talk theology again, aren't you?"

"Probably." They both laughed. He felt almost gay. He loved arguing, particularly when he could argue on the obsessive topic of the structure of the mind.

If they were going to mind again, now was clearly the time to do it, while they were in some sort of accord. Mind-travel was never easy, and the passage could be rough if one was emotionally upset.

They packed their bags and strapped their few possessions to themselves. Then they linked themselves together, arm in arm; otherwise, there was no guarantee they would not arrive a few million years and several hundred miles apart from each other.

They broke open their drug packs. The CSD came in little ampoules, clear, almost colourless. Held up to the wide Palaeozoic sky, Bush's ampoule showed slightly green between his fingers. They looked at each other; Ann made a face and they swallowed together.

Bush felt the cryptic acid run down his throat. The liquid was a symbol of the hydrosphere, sacrificial wine to represent the oceans from which life had come, oceans that still washed in the arteries of man, oceans that still regulated and made habitable his external world, oceans that still provided food and climate, oceans that were the blood of the biosphere.

And he himself was a biosphere, containing all the fossil lives and ideas of his ancestors, containing other life forms, containing countless untold possibilities, containing life and death.

He was an analogue of the world; through the CSD, he could translate from one form to the other.

Only in the transitional state, as the drug took effect, could one begin to grasp the nature of the minute energy-duration disturbance that the solar system represented. That system, a bubble within a sea of cosmic forces, as part of a meta-structure that was boundless but not infinite with respect to both time and space. And this banal fact had become astonishing to man only because man had shut himself off from it, had shielded his mind from the immensity of it as the ionosphere round his planet shielded him from harmful radiations, had lost that knowledge, had defended himself from that knowledge with the concept of passing time, that managed to make the universe tolerable by cutting off – not only the immense size of it, as recent generations had rediscovered – but the immense time of it. Immense time had been chopped into tiny wriggling fragments that man could deal with, could trap with sundials, sandglasses, pocket watches, grandfather clocks, chronometers, which succeeded generation by generation in shaving time down finer and finer, smaller and smaller...until the obsessive nature of the whole procedure had been recognized, and Wenlock and his fellow workers blew the gaff on the whole conspiracy.

But the conspiracy had been necessary. Without it, unsheltered from the blind desert of space-time, man would still be with the other animals, wandering in tribes by the rim of the echoing Quaternary seas. Or so the theory went. At least it was clear there had been a conspiracy.

Now the shield was down. The complexities of the cerebrum and cerebellum were naked to the co-continuous universe and were devouring all they came across.

Minding was a momentary process. It looked easy, although there was rigorous training behind it. As the CSD tilted their metabolisms, Bush and Ann went into the discipline – that formula the Institute had devised for guiding them through the prohibitions of the human mind. The Devonian dissolved now, appearing to be a huge marching creature of duration, with spatial characteristics serving simply as an exoskeleton. Bush opened his mouth to laugh, but no sound came. In the exhilaration of travel, one lost most physical characteristics. Everything seemed to go, except the sense of direction. It was like swimming against a current; the difficult way was towards one's own "present"; to drift into the remote past was relatively easy – and led to eventual death by suffocation, as many had found. If a foetus in the womb were granted the ability to mind-travel, it would be faced with much the same situation: either to battle forward to the climactic moment of birth, or to sink easefully back to the final — or was it first — moment of non-existence.

He was not aware of duration, or of the pulse within him that served as his chronometer. In a strange hypnoid state, he felt only a sense of being near to a great body of reality that seemed to bear as much kinship to God as to Earth. And he caught himself trying to laugh again.

Then the laughter died, and he felt he was in flight. Ages rolled below him like night. He was aware of the discomfort of having someone with him — and then he and Ann were surrounded by a dark green world, and reality as it was generally experienced was about them again.

Jurassic reality.

chapter three

at the sign of the amniote egg

Bush had never liked the Jurassic. It was too hot and cloudy, and reminded him of one long and miserable day in his childhood when, caught doing something innocently naughty, he had been shut out in the garden all day by his mother. It had been cloudy that day too, with the heat so heavy the butterflies had hardly been able to fly above flower-top level.

Ann let go of him and stretched. They had materialized beside a dead tree. Its bare shining arms were like a reproof to the girl; Bush realized for the first time what a slut she was, how dirty and unkempt, and wondered why it did not alter what he felt about her – whatever that might precisely be.

Not speaking, they moved forward, full of the sense of disorientation that always followed mind-travel. There was no rational way of knowing whereabouts or whenabouts on Earth they were; yet an irrational part of the undermind knew, and would gradually come through with the information. It, after all, had brought them here, and presumably for purposes of its own.

They were in the foothills of mountains on which jungle rioted. Halfway up the mountain slopes, the clouds licked away everything from sight. All was still; the foliage about them seemed frozen in a long Mesozoic hush.

"We'd better move down into the plain," Bush said. "This is the place we want, I think. I have friends here, the Borrows."

"They live here, you mean?"

"They run a store. Roger Borrow used to be an artist. His wife's nice."

"Will I like them?"

"I shouldn't think so."

He started walking. Not knowing clearly what he felt about Ann, he thought that presenting her to Roger and Ver might cement a relationship he did not want. Ann watched him for a while and then followed. The Jurassic was about the most boring place to be alone in ever devised.

With their packs on their backs, they spent most of the day climbing downwards. It was not easy because they could never see their footholds; they were wailed off completely from the reality all round them. They were spectres, unable to alter by the slightest degree the humblest appurtenances of this world – unable to kick the smallest pebble out of the way – unless it was that by haunting it they altered the charisma of the place. Only the air-leakers gave them some slight bond with actuality, by drawing their air requirements through the invisible wall of time-entropy about them. The level of the generalized floor on which they trod was sometimes below the "present" level of the ground, so that they trudged along up to their spectral knees in the dirt; or at another time they appeared to be stepping on air.

In the forest they were able to walk straight through the trees. But an occasional tree would stop them; they felt it as a marsh-mallowy presence and had to go round it; for its lifespan would be long enough – it would survive the hazards of life long enough – to create a shadowy obstruction in their path.

When sunset was drawing near, Bush stopped and pitched his tent, pumping until it struggled into position. He and the girl ate together, and then he washed himself rather ostentatiously as they prepared for sleep.

"Don't you ever wash?" he asked.

"Sometimes. I suppose you wash to please yourself?"

"Who else?"

"I stay grubby to please myself."

"It must be some sort of neurosis."

"Yes. Probably it's because it always annoys clean blighters like you."

He sat down by her and looked into her face. "You really want to annoy people, do you? Why? Is it because you think it's good for them? Or good for you?"

"Maybe it's because I've given up hoping to please them."

"I've always thought people were on the whole pathetically easy to please." Later, when he recalled that fragment of conversation, he was annoyed that he had not paid more attention to her remark; undoubtedly it offered an insight into Ann's behaviour, and perhaps a clue as to how she could best be treated. But by that time he had come to the conclusion that for all her prickliness she was a girl one could genuinely converse with – and she was gone.

He was wrong in any case to challenge her after she had gone though a tiring day so uncomplainingly; even the Dark Woman had faded off duty.

He woke next morning to find Ann still asleep, and staggered out to look at the dawn. It was like a dream to climb from bed and find the great overloaded landscape outside; but the dream was capable of sustaining itself for millions of years. A million years...perhaps by a scale of values of which mankind might one day be master, a million years would be seen as more meaningless, more trivial, than a second. In the same way, not one of these dawns could have as much effect on him as the most insignificant remark Ann might drop.

As they were packing up to move on, she asked him again if he was going to do a groupage of her. Bush was glad of even uninformed interest in his work.

"I'm looking for something new to do. I'm at a block – it's a familiar thing for creative artists. Suddenly human consciousness is lumbered with this entirely new time structure, and I want to reflect it as best I can in my creative work –

without just doing an illustration, if you understand. But I can't begin, can't begin to begin."

"Are you going to do a groupage of me?"

"I just told you: no. Groupages aren't portraits of particular people."

"They're abstracts, I gather?"

"You don't know J M W Turner's work do you! Ever since his day – he was a mid-Victorian – we've had technical ways of reproducing the forms of nature. Abstracts reproduce forms of ideas; and, for all our computers, only man can make abstracts."

"I love computer-pictures."

"I hate them. My spatial-kinetic groupages try to…oh, identify the spirit of a moment, an age. Sometimes, I used to work in mirror-glass – then everyone saw an SKG differently, with fragments of their own features lurking over it. That's the way we see the universe. There's no such thing as an objective view of the universe – ever think of that? Our features look back at us from every quarter."

"Are you religious, Bush?"

He shook his head and stood up slowly, looking away from her. "I wish I was religious. My father, he's a dentist, he's a religious man… Yet sometimes, when I was successful the ideas were really pouring out of my fingers, doing my best SKGs, I knew I had a bit of God in me."

At the mention of God, they both became self-conscious. As he helped Ann up, Bush said in curt, workaday tones, "So you don't know Turner's work?"

That closed the subject.

Not until the afternoon, as they were coming down on to the plains, did they see the first creatures of the plains, sporting in a valley. Instinct asserting itself, Bush's impulse was to watch them from behind a tree. Then he recalled they were less than ghosts to these bulky creatures, and walked out into the open towards them. Ann followed.

Eighteen stegosauri seemed to fill the small valley. The male was a giant, perhaps twenty feet long and round as a barrel, his spiky armour making him appear much larger than he was. The chunky plates along his backbone were a dull slaty green, but much of his body armour was a livid orange. He tore at foliage with his jaws, but perpetually kept his beady eyes alert for danger.

He had two females with him. They were smaller than he, and more lightly armoured. One in particular was prettily marked, the plates of her spine being almost the same light yellow as her underbelly.

About the stegosauri frisked their young. Bush and Ann walked among them, absolutely immune. There were fifteen of them, and obviously not many weeks hatched. Unencumbered as yet by more than the lightest vestige of armour, they skipped about their mothers like lambs, often standing on their tall hind legs, sometimes jumping over their parents' wickedly spiked tails.

The two humans stood in the middle of the herd, watching the antics of the young reptiles.

"Maybe that's why those things became extinct," Ann said. "The young ones all got hooked on jumping their mothers' tails and spiked themselves to death!"

"It's as good as any other theory to date."

Only then did he notice the intruder, although the old man stegosaur had been backing about puffily for some while. From a nearby thicket, another animal was watching the scene. Bush took Ann's arm and directed her attention to the spot. As he did so, the bushes parted and another stegosaurus emerged. This was a male, smaller and presumably younger than the leader of the herd, his tail swishing from side to side.

The females and the young paid only the most cursory attention to the intruder; the females continued to munch, the youngsters to play. The leader immediately charged forward to deal with the intruder; he was being challenged for possession of the herd.

Travelling smartly towards each other, the two males hit, shoulder to shoulder. To the humans it was entirely soundless. The great beasts stood there absorbing the shock, and then slowly pressed forward until they were side by side, one facing one way, one the other. They began to heave at each other, using their tails for leverage but never as weapons. Their mouths opened, they displayed little sharp teeth. Still the females and their young showed no interest in what was happening.

The males strained and struggled, their legs bowed until their ungainly bodies almost touched the ground. The older animal was winning by sheer weight. Suddenly, the intruder was forced to take a step backwards. The leader nearly fell on to him. They stood apart. For a moment, the intruder looked back at the females, his mouth hanging open. Then he lumbered off into the nearby thicket and was not seen again.

After a few snorts of triumph, the leader of the little herd returned to his females. They looked up, then resumed their placid munching.

"A lot they care what happens to him!" Bush said.

"They've probably learnt by now that there's not much to choose between one male and another."

He looked sharply at her. She was grinning. He softened, and smiled back.

When they climbed out of the far end of the valley, they had a wide panorama of the plains with a river meandering through them. Great forests started again a mile or two away. Close at hand, situated on a long outcrop of rock, was the Borrows' tent, and other signs of human habitation.

"At least we can get a drink," Ann said, as they approached the motley collection of tents.

"You go ahead. I want to stay here for a while and think." Bush still had his head stuffed full of dinosaurs. They disturbed him. Morally? Two men disputing over women rarely showed as little vindictiveness as those great armoured vegetarians. Aesthetically? Who could say what beauty was, except from his own standpoint? In any case, that great spinal column, rising to its highest point over the pelvis and then dying away in the spiked tail, had its own unassailable logic. Intellectually? He thought of Lenny, and then diverted his attention back to the sportive reptilian young, so full of wit in their movements.

He squatted on the spongy floor, which here corresponded almost exactly with a boulder, and watched Ann walking away from him. He overcame an impulse to pluck a nearby leaf and chew it; vegetation here was unpluckable by any ghostly fingers.

One of the most curious effects of mind-travel was the diminution of light suffered by anyone out of their proper time. Only a few yards away, Ann was already in deep shadow and the Borrows' bar, although white-painted, was even gloomier. But there were other shades here that added not merely gloom but horror to the scene. Borrow had chosen what was evidently a popular site. Future generations of mind-travellers would also congregate here; it would become a town – perhaps the first Jurassic town. The signs of its future success were all around. Spectral figures of future buildings and people could be seen, drabber and mistier as they were farther in the future.

Bush was sitting close to a building very much superior to the tents of his own generation. By its degree of slaty shade, so transparent that he could see the unkempt landscape through it, he judged it to emanate from a time perhaps a century or more ahead of his own. Those future beings had solved many of the problems that in these early days of mind-travel seemed utterly baffling: for instance, the transportation of heavy materials and the installation of electric plants. The future had moved in to live in style in the remote past; Bush's present could do no more than camp like savages here.

They would also have solved the problem of sewage; his generation was leaving its excreta strewn from the Pleistocene to the Cambrian without the hope or excuse that it would ever turn into coprolites.

From the future building, people were leaning. So faintly were they drawn in the air, it was impossible to be sure if they were men or women. He had that disturbing feeling that their eyes were slightly brighter than they should be. They could see him no better than he could see them, but the sensation of being overlooked was uncomfortable. Bush turned his gaze away towards the plain, only to realize how covered it was with the misty obstructions of future time. Two faint phantasms of men walked through him, deep in conversation, not a decibel of which leaked though the time-entropy barrier to him. He had already noticed that his shadow woman was near him again; how did she feel about Ann? Ghost though she was, she would have feelings, there in her stifling future. The whole of space-time was becoming stuffed with human feelings. Briefly, he thought again of Monet. The old boy was right to concentrate on water lilies; they might overgrow their pond, but you never caught them swarming over the bank and the nearby trees as well.

He recalled Borrow had been a painter, back in their youth. Borrow would be a good man to talk to. Borrow was hard-hearted, but he could sometimes make you laugh.

As he got up and strolled towards his friend's establishment, he saw that Borrow had very much improved the amenities. There were three tents instead of the pair there had been, and two of them were considerable in size. One was a sort of general-store-cum-trading post, one was a bar, one was a café. Over them all, Borrow and his wife had hoisted a great sign: THE AMNIOTE EGG.

Behind the tents, before them, amid them, were other collections of buildings in strange styles of architecture, some of them also called THE AMNIOTE EGG, all of them in various degrees of shadow, according to their degrees of futurity. It had been the presence of these shadows, so clearly omens of success, that had encouraged the Borrows to set up business in the first place; they were flourishing on the paradox.

"Two amniote egg and chips," Bush said, as he pushed his way into the café.

Ver was behind the counter. Her hair was greyer than Bush remembered it; she would be about fifty. She smiled her old smile and came out from behind the counter to shake Bush's hand. He noted that her hand felt glassy; they had not mind-travelled back from the same year; the same effect made her face greyer, shadier than it really was. Even her voice came muted, drained away by the slight time-barrier. He knew that the food and drink, when he took it, would have the same "Glassy" quality and digest slowly.

They chaffed each other affectionately, and Bush said the old place was clearly making Ver's fortune.

"Bet you don't even know what an amniote egg is," Ver said. Her parents had christened her Verbena, but she preferred the contraction.

"It means big business to you, doesn't it?"

"We're keeping body and soul together. And you, Eddie? Your body looks all right – how's the soul doing?"

"Still getting trouble from it." He had known this woman well in the days when he and Borrow were struggling painters, before mind-travel, had even slept with her once or twice before Roger had become seriously interested. It all seemed a long while ago – about a hundred and thirty million years ago, or ahead, whichever it was. Sometimes past and future became confused and seemed to flow in opposite directions to normal. "Don't seem to get as many signals from it as I used to, but those that do come through are mainly bad."

"Can't they operate?"

"Doc says it's incurable." It was marvellous how he could talk so trivially to her about such momentous things. "Talking of incurables, how's Roger?"

"He's okay. You'll find him out back. You doing any grouping nowadays, Eddie?"

"Well – I'm just in a sort of transition stage. I'm – hell, no, Ver, I'm absolutely lost at the moment." He might as well tell her an approximation of the truth; she was the only woman who asked about his work because she actually cared what he did.

"Lost periods are sometimes necessary. You're doing nothing?"

"Did a couple of paintings last time I was in 2090. Just to pass the time. Structuring time, psychologists call it. There's a theory that man's biggest problem is structuring time. All wars are merely part-solutions to the problem."

"The Hundred Years War would rate as quite a success in that case."

"Yep. It puts all art, all music, all literature, into that same category. All time-passers, Lear, the St Matthew Passion, Guernica, Sinning in the City."

"The difference is one of degree presumably."

"It's the degrees I'm up against right now."

They exchanged smiles. He pressed into the back to find Borrow. For the first time – or had he felt the same thing before and forgotten it? – he thought that Ver was more interesting than her husband.

Borrow was puttering about outside in the grey daylight. Like his wife, he was inclining to stoutness, but he still dressed as immaculately as ever, with the old hint of the dandy about him. He straightened as Bush came across to him and held out a hand.

"Haven't seen you in a million years, Eddie. How's life? Do you still hold the record for low-distance mind-travel?"

"As far as I know, Roger. How're you doing?"

"What's the nearest year to home you ever reached?"

"There were men about." He did not get the drift of, or see the necessity for, his friend's question.

"That's pretty good. Could you date it?"

"It was some time in the Bronze Age." Of course, everyone who minded was fascinated by the idea that, when the discipline was developed further, it might be possible for them to visit historic times. Who knows, the day might even dawn when it would be possible to break through the entropy barrier entirely and mind into the future.

Borrow slapped him on the back. "Good going! See any artists at work? We had a chap in the bar the other day claimed he had minded up to the Stone Age. I thought that was pretty good, but evidently you still hold the record."

"Yeah, well, they say it needs a disrupted personality to get as far as I got!"

They looked into each other's eyes. Borrow dropped his gaze almost at once. Perhaps he recalled that Bush hated being touched. The latter, regretting his outburst, made an effort to pull himself together and be pleasant.

"Nice to see you and Ver again. Looks as if The Amniote Egg is doing well. And — Roger, you're painting again!" He had noticed what Borrow was stacking. He stooped, and gently lifted one of the plasbord panels into the light.

There were nine panels. Bush looked through them all in growing amazement.

"You've taken up your old hobby again," he said thickly.

"Poaching a bit on your territory, I'm afraid, Eddie."

But these were not SKGs. These panels seemed to look back, in one sense, to Gabo and Pevsner, but using the new materials, here etiolated, here compounded; the effect was startlingly new, not sculpture, not groupage, not machine.

All nine panels were variations on a theme, encrusted, as Bush saw, with perspex and glass, and with rotating fragments of metal held in place by electro-magnets. They were so formed that they carried suggestions of great distances, with relationships that varied according to the point from which they were viewed. Some were in continual movement, powered by pill-thrust from micro-miniaturized nuclear drives set in the panel bases, so that the static element had been eliminated.

It was immediately clear to Bush what the groupages represented: abstractions of the time strata folded so ominously about The Amniote Egg. They had been created with absolute clarity and command – command of vision and material, coalescing to produce masterworks. Hard after Bush's awe came his jealousy burning through him like a flood.

"Very cute," he said, expressionlessly.

"I thought *you* might understand them," Borrow said, staring hard into his friend's face.

"I came here after a girl I know. I want a drink!"

"Have one on the house. Your girl may be in the bar."

He led the way and Bush followed, too angry to speak. The panels were astonishing – cool, yet with a Dionysiac quality – revolutionary, selective, individual…they gave Bush that prickle between his shoulder blades which he recognized as his private signal when something had genius; or if not genius, a quality he might imitate and perhaps transmute into genius, whatever the hell genius was – a stronger prickle, a greater surge of electricity through the cells of the body. And old Borrow had it, *Borrow*, who had stopped being any sort of artist years ago and turned himself into a shopkeeper and his pretty wife into an assistant for the sake of cash, *Borrow*, fussy about his shirt cuffs, *Borrow* had got the message and delivered it back!

What hurt was that Borrow knew he had done it. That was why he had tried to cushion Bush from the shock by reminding him that he held the record for low-distance mind-travel. Bush might be washed up as an artist, ah, but he held the record for low-distance mind-travel! So Borrow had known Bush would recognize the merits of the panels and had pitied him because he (Bush) could produce nothing similar.

How much were those panels fetching in 2090, for God's sake? No wonder The Amniote Egg was flourishing; there was capital to back it now. The shopkeeper artist was on a good thing, turning his inspiration into hamburgers and tonic water!

Bush hated his thoughts. They kept coming, though he called himself a bastard. Those panels...of course... Gabo... Pevsner...in two dimensions – no, they had their predecessors, but these were originals. Not a new language, but a bridge from the old. A bridge he himself might have found; now he would find another, have to find another! But old Borrow... A man who'd once dared to laugh at Turner's masterpieces!

"Double whisky," Bush said. He couldn't pull himself together to say thank you as Borrow sat down on a stool companionably beside him.

"Is your girl here? What's she like? Blonde?"

"She's dirty. God knows what colour her hair is. Picked her up in the Devonian. She's no good – I'm only too glad to lose her." It was not true; in his shame he could not think what he was saying. Already, he wanted to look at the panels again, but was unable to ask.

Borrow sat in silence for a moment, as if digesting how much of Bush's statement he should believe. Then he said, "You still work for the Wenlock Institute, Eddie?"

"Yes. Why?"

"Guy in here yesterday called Stein – must still be around. He used to work for Wenlock too."

"Don't know him." *That* Stein connected with the Institute? Never!

"Need a room for the night, Eddie? Ver and I can fix you up."

"I've got my own tent. Anyhow, I may not be staying."

"Come on, you must have a meal with Ver and me, tonight after we've closed. There's no hurry – there's all the world in the time, as they say."

"Can't." He made an awful effort to pull himself together and stop being a bastard. "What the hell is an amniote egg anyway? A new dish?"

"You could say that in a way." Borrow explained the amniote egg as the great invention of the Mesozoic Era, the one thing that brought about the dominance of the great reptiles over hundreds of millions of years. An amnion was the membrane within a reptilian egg that allowed the embryo reptile to go through the "tadpole" stage inside the egg, to emerge into the world as a fully formed creature. It enabled the reptiles to lay their eggs on land, and thus conquer the continents. For the amphibians from which they had developed laid only soft and gelatinous eggs that had to hatch in a fluid medium, which kept them pegged to rivers and lakes.

"The reptiles broke the old amphibian tie with the water as surely as mankind broke the old mammal tie with space-time time. It was their big clever trick, and it stood them in good stead for I-don't-know-how-long."

"The way your store and bar is going to do for you."

'What's upset you, Eddie, boy? You're not yourself? You ought to go back to the present."

Bush drained his glass, stood up, and looked at his friend. With a great effort, he conquered himself. "I may be back, Roger. I thought – your constructions were okay." As he hurried out of the bar he saw there was one of the constructions hanging as decoration on the canvas wall.

All the clocks of his mind were hammering furiously. You ought to be glad someone did it. Christ, you ought to be glad your friend did it. But I've suffered... Maybe he suffered – maybe he suffers all the time like me – you never can tell. He hasn't done anything. Those were just flashy tourist gimmicks. I'm so despicable. You've no control over yourself. All this self-recrimination is itself just a cover-up. And beneath that and beneath that – go on peeling the layers away and you'll see they always come alternate, self-love and self-hate, right down to the rotten core. It's my parents' fault... Incest motif again. God, I'm so sick of myself! Let me out!

He saw how he had wasted himself. Five years before, he had been doing good work. Now he was just a spineless mind-travel addict.

One of the ways of escape from himself was to hand. A man and a girl were walking in front of him, so unshadowed that Bush knew they had come back from the same year as he. He hardly glanced at the man. The girl was terrific, with beautiful legs and a sort of high-stepping walk that suited her trim ankles. Her bottom was good and did not slope too much. Her hair was short. Bush could see nothing of her face, but to look at it immediately became his obsession.

It was a gambler's urge of which he had long been victim — and now he no longer had the excuse that he needed a model. The odds were stacked high against any girl being a beauty. A thousand girls had pretty posteriors — one in a thousand had a tolerable face. The fever died in him directly he found one that did not match up to his standards. He was a face fetishist. Even as he fell into pursuit, Bush realized — it was an aside — Ann had a pretty face.

He followed the couple carefully, moving from side to side behind the girl, so that by this liberation he could see the maximum amount of her profile. There were tents pitched here, and ragged individuals standing about, wondering what the devil to do with the past now they had it. Bush avoided them.

His quarry disappeared round the corner of a tent. Quickening his pace, Bush followed. He saw the girl was standing alone just ahead. She had turned to look at him. She was a cow. Almost at the same moment, Bush scented danger. He whirled about, but the blow was already descending. The girl's escort had jumped out of the tent doorway, and was bringing a cosh down over his shoulder, hard.

The moment stretched into a whole season, as if the panic in Bush's mind had flushed it of the man-made idea of passing time. He had more than enough leisure to read the fear and madness — as hateful as the dreaded blow itself — in the man's face, and to perform a whole series of connected observations: I should have looked at the man, or at least have spared him a glance: I recognize him: he was that odd fellow with Lenny and Ann, blast her: dyed hair; his name was – but Roger mentioned the name too: why didn't I take it in? why am I always so involved in something else? always something egotistic, of course: now I'm for trouble; Stone – no, Stein. Stein, Stein!

The cosh landed, clumsily but hard, half across his face and half across his neck. He went down. Anger came to him too late (again because he was too self-involved to react quickly to the external situation?) and as he felt he grappled for Stein's legs. His fingers clutched trousers. Stein kicked him in the chest and pulled away. Sprawling on the soggy, generalized floor, Bush saw the man run away, past the girl, not bothering about her.

The whole incident had not raised even one grain of Jurassic dust. It remained alien, unstirrable.

Two men came over and helped Bush up. They said something about helping him over to The Amniote Egg. That was the last thing he wanted. Still in a daze, he snatched himself away from them and staggered off, moving out of the tented area, clutching his neck, all his emotions jarring and churning inside him. He remembered the girl's face as she turned to watch him collect his come-uppance: with her heavy brows and silly little nose, she had not been even near to pretty.

Where the crude tents of his own day finished, the shadowy structures belonging to future invaders of the past continued. Bush lurched through them, through the shadows that inhabited them, finally got beyond them and pushed through a green thicket of gymnosperms. A little coelurosaur, no bigger than a hen, and scuttling on its hind legs, ran out from under his feet. It startled him, although he had not caused its fright.

Emerging from the thicket, he found himself on the bank of a wide and slow-moving river, the one he and Ann had seen before she left him. He sat by it with a hand over his throbbing neck. There was jungle close at hand, the heavy, almost flowerless jungle of mid-Jurassic times, while, on the opposite side of the river, where an ox-bow was forming, it was marshy and bulrushes and barrel-bodied cycadeoids flourished.

Bush stared at the scene for some moments, wondering what he was thinking about it, until he realized it reminded him of a picture in a textbook, long ago, when he was at school, before the days of mind-travel but when – curiously, as it now seemed – a general preoccupation with the remote past was evident. That would be about 2056, when his father opened his new dentist's surgery. People had gone Victoriana-mad during that period – his father had even installed a plastic mahogany rinse-bowl for people to spit into. It was the Victorians who had first revealed the world of prehistory, with its monsters so like the moving things in the depths of the mind, and presumably one thing had led to another. Presumably Wenlock had been influenced by the same currents of the period. But Wenlock had turned out to be the first mind of his age, not a beaten-up failed artist.

The picture in the textbook long ago, had had the same arrangement of river, marsh, various plants of exotic kinds, and distant forest which now stretched before Bush. Only the picture had also exhibited a selection of prime reptiles: one allosaurus large on the left of the picture, picking in a refined way at an overturned stegosaurus; next, a comptosaurus, walking like a man with its little front paws raised almost as if it were about to pray for the soul of the stegosaurus; its devotions were interrupted by two pterodactyls swooping about in the middle of the picture; then came a little fleet-foot ornitholestes, grabbing an archaeopteryx out of a fern; and lastly, on the right of the picture, a brontosaurus obligingly thrust its long neck and head out of the river, weed hanging neatly out of its mouth to indicate its vegetarian habit.

How simple the world of the textbook, how like and unlike reality! This creaking old green world was never as crowded as the textbooks claimed; nor could the animals, any more than the man, exist in such single blessedness. Nor, for that matter, had

Bush ever seen a pterodactyl. Perhaps they were scarce. Perhaps they inhabited another part of the globe. Or perhaps it was just that some imaginative nineteenth-century paleontologist had fitted the fossil bones of some crawling creature together wrongly. The pterodactyl could be purely a Victorian invention, one with Peter Pan, Alice in Wonderland, and Dracula.

It was hot and cloudy – that at least squared with the picture, for none of the animals there had cast shadows – much like the day his mother had said she did not love him and proved her point by shutting him out in the garden all day. He now longed for a good old friendly brontosaurus head to come champ-champ-champing out of the river; it might have done him some good on that other day, too; but no brontosaurus appeared. The truth was, the Age of Reptiles was never quite so overcrowded with reptiles as the Age of Man with men.

As the pain within him died and his pulse rate slowed to normal, Bush made some attempt to ratiocinate. Guilt kept slipping into his reasoning but begot some things clear.

Stein, for whatever cause, had clearly believed Bush was following him rather than the girl. If Stein was about here, it was likely that Lenny and his buckskin-coated chums would also be around. Their presence might account for the disappearance of Ann; Lenny could have caught her and be holding her against her will. No, be your age, she had seen him and run to him with thankfulness, only too glad to exchange his dirty feet and dim mind for Bush's pretentious chatter. Well, good riddance to her! Though by God, that first evening, across the uncrunching phragmoceras shells, in that little valley, her gesture in raising one crooked leg, the exquisite planes of her thighs, and their sweet creaming excitement...

"Don't get all worked up!" he exclaimed aloud. Another thing was clear. He did not want anything from anyone here, not from Roger and Ver, not from Lenny and his tershers, not from Stein. But it was possible that one or more of them might follow him and beat him up. As for Ann…he had no claims on her. He had done nothing good for her.

Bush looked anxiously about. Even the dark woman had left him. It was time for him to mind home, to face the trouble at the Institute. The Jurassic, as ever, was a flop, it and its amniote eggs.

He opened his pack and pulled out an ampoule of CSD. His old, ancient, long-ago, present was awaiting for him. No reptiles there. Only parents.

chapter four

it takes more than death

Mind-travel was easy in some circumstances, once its principles and the Wenlock discipline were learnt. But to return to the present was as full of pain and effort as birth. It was a rebirth. Blackness hemmed one, claustrophobia threatened, the danger of suffocation was immediate. Bush kicked and struggled and cried with his mind. "There, that place!" directing himself forward with the peristaltic movements of some unknown part of his brain.

Light returned to his universe. He sprawled on a yielding couch, and luxury pervaded his being; he was back. Slowly, he opened his eyes. He was back in the Southall mind-station from which he had come. His neck still hurt, but he was home.

He lay in a sort of cocoon in a cubicle that would have remained unopened since he left, one winter's day in 2090. Above his head was the small plant keeping alive some of his tissue and a quarter-pint of his blood. They were almost his only possessions in this age, certainly his most vital ones, for on them, by some awesome osmotic process, he had been able to home like a homing pigeon. Now their usefulness was over.

Bush sat up, tore away the fine plastic skin that cocooned the bed – it was reminiscent of a dinosaur rolling out of its damned amniote egg, wasn't it? – and surveyed his cubicle. A calendar-clock on the wall gave him the dry fact of the date: Tuesday, 2nd

April 2093. He had not meant to be away so long; there was always a sensation of being robbed of life when you returned and found how time had been ticking on without you. For the past was not the real world; it was just a dream, like the future; it was the present that was real, the present of passing time which man had invented, and with which he was stuck.

Climbing out of his pack, Bush stood up and surveyed himself in the mirror. Amid these sanitary surroundings, he looked scruffy and filthy. He fed his measurements into the clotheomat and dialled for a one-piece. It was delivered in thirty seconds flat; a metal drawer containing it sprang open and caught Bush painfully on the shin. He took the garment out, laid it on the bed, removed his wrist instruments, picked up a clean towel from the heated rail, and padded into the shower. As he roused himself in the warm water – unimaginable luxury – he thought of Ann and her grubby flesh, lost somewhere back in a time that was now transmuted into layers of broken rock, buried underground. From now on, he would have to regard her as just another of his casual lays; there was no reason to suppose he would ever see her again.

In ten minutes, he was fit to leave the cubicle. He rang the bell, and a male attendant came to unlock the door and present him with a bill for room and services. Bush stared at the amount and winced: but the Wenlock Institute would pay that. He would have to report there shortly, prove that he had been doing something in the last two and a half years. First, he would go home and be the dutiful son. Anything to delay the report a little.

Slinging his pack over one shoulder, he walked down the spotless corridor – behind those locked doors so many other escapees foraged through their minds into the dark backward and abysm of time – into the entrance hall. One of his groupages was there, one of the largest, bolted on to the ceiling. Bloody Borrow had superseded it. Forbidding himself to look up at it, he went over towards the heat baffles and stepped into the open.

"Taxshaw, sir?"

"Going-home present, sir? Lovely little dollies!"

"Buy some flowers, mister – daffs fresh picked today."

"Taxshaw! Take you anywhere!"

"Want a girl, squire? Take your mind off mind-travel?"

"Spare a cent!"

He remembered the cries of despair. This was home; 2090 or 2093, this was the time track he knew. He could make a textbook picture of it, the unfortunates ranged from left to right, like dinosaurs in the other diagram: male beggar first, then female, then taxshawman pulling his carriage, then toy-vendor, clouting away ragged kid, with flower-woman extreme right, under lamp-post; and in the background, the smart mind-station contrasted with the filthy ragged houses and broken roads. Jostling his way through the little knot of mendicants and hawkers, he started to walk, changed his mind, and went over to a taxshawman sitting sullenly in his carriage. Giving his father's address, he asked how much the ride would cost. The man told him.

"It's far too much!"

"Prices have gone up while you've been flitting round the past."

They always said that. It was always true.

Bush climbed into the vehicle, the man lifted the shafts, and they were off.

The air tasted wonderful! It was a miracle that only this tiny sliver of time, the present, should seem to have the magical stuff in abundance, everywhere, even where there were no people. Clever devices though the air-leakers were, they always made one feel near to suffocation. And it was not only air – there were a thousand sounds here, all striking blessedly on Bush's ear, even the harsh ones. Also, everything that could be seen had its individual tactile quality; everything that had been turned to rubbery glass in the past here possessed its own miraculous properties of texture.

Although he knew he was thoroughly hooked on mind-travel, and would inevitably plunge back again, he loathed the abdication of the senses it entailed. Here was the world, the real world – rattling, blazing, living: and probably a little too much for him, as it had proved before!

Already, as he filled his lungs, as they rattled through the streets, could see disturbing signs that 2093 was far from being a paradise, perhaps even farther from being a paradise than 2090. Maybe the adage was right that said you could stay away too long; perhaps already the mindless reptilian past was more familiar than this present. He knew he did not really belong here when he could not understand the slogans scrawled on the brick walls.

At one point, a column of soldiers in double file marched down the road. The taxshawman gave them a wide berth.

"Trouble in town?"

"Not if you keep your nose clean."

An ambiguous answer, Bush thought.

He took some while to grasp exactly why the road in which his parents lived looked smaller, baser, altogether more drab. It was not just because several windows had been broken and boarded up; that he recalled from before, and the litter in the streets. It was only as he paid off the man and confronted his father's house that he realized all the trees in the road had been chopped down. In the dentist's neat little front garden, two ornamental cherries had grown – James Bush had planted them himself when he first took over the practice – they would have been coming into blossom about now. As he walked up the brick path, he saw their brown and decaying stumps sticking out of the ground like advertisements for his father's profession.

Some things were the same. The brass plate still announced James Bush, LDS, Dental Surgeon. Tucked into a transparent plastic holder, the card still said "Please Ring and Walk In" in his mother's handwriting. As the practice went downhill, she had been forced for economic reasons to become her husband's receptionist, thus providing an unwitting example of time's turning full circle, since it was as his receptionist she had got to know him in the first place. Bush braced himself to hear a flood of examples of how things had gone farther downhill since he left; his mother was always expert at providing tedious and repetitive examples of anything. Grasping the doorknob, he Walked In Without Ringing.

The hall, which was also the waiting-room, was empty. Magazines and newspapers lay about on table and chairs, notices, diagrams and certificates crowded the walls, rather as if this were a centre for testing literacy.

"Mother!" he called, looking up the stairs. It was gloomy up on the landing. There was no movement.

He did not call his mother again. Instead, he tapped on the surgery door and walked in.

His father, Jimmy Bush, James Bush, LDS, sat in the dental chair gazing out into his back garden. He wore carpet slippers, and his white smock was unbuttoned, to reveal a ragged pullover underneath. He looked round slowly at his son, as though reluctant to regard one more human being.

"Hello, Father! It's me again – I've just got back."

"Ted, my boy! We'd given you up! Fancy seeing you! So you've come back, have you?"

"Yes, Father." For some situations, there were no rational forms of speech.

Jimmy Bush climbed out of the chair and shook his son's hand, grinning as they muttered affectionately at each other. He was of the same build as his son, a rather untidy figure. Age and habit had endowed him with a slightly apologetic stoop, and the same hint of apology appeared in his smile. Jimmy Bush was not a man who claimed very much for himself.

"I thought you were never coming back! This needs celebrating! I've got a little something over here. Scotch mouthwash – dentist's ruin." He fumbled in a cupboard, shifted a sterilizer, and brought forth a half-empty half-bottle of whisky.

"Know how much this costs now, Ted? Fifty pounds sixty cents, and that's just half a bottle. It went up again at the last budget. Oh, I don't know what things are coming to, really I don't! You know what Wordsworth said – 'The world is too much with us, late and soon, Getting and spending we lay waste our powers.' He'd have a fit if he were alive today!"

Bush had forgotten his father's literary tags. He enjoyed them. Trying to infuse some life into himself, he said, "I only just got back, Dad. Haven't even reported to the Institute yet." As his father brought two glasses out, he asked, "Is mother in?"

Jimmy Bush hesitated, then busied himself pouring out the whisky. "Your mother died last June, Ted. June the Tenth. She'd been ill several months. She often asked after you. Of course, we were very sorry you weren't here, but there was nothing we could do, was there?"

"No. No, nothing. Dad, I'm sorry…I never… Was it anything bad?" Realizing the idiocy of what he was saying, he corrected himself. "I mean, what was the trouble?"

"The usual," Jimmy Bush said, as if his wife had often died before; his attention was straying to his glass, which he lifted eagerly, "Cancer poor old girl. But it was in the bowels, and she never had a moment's pain with it, so we must be thankful. Well, cheers anyway – good health!"

Bush hardly knew how to respond. His mother had never been a happy woman, but memories of some of her happy hours crowded back on him now, most poignantly. He took a drink of whisky. It was neat and tasted like some sort of disinfectant, but its course down his throat was gratifying. He accepted a mescahale when his father offered him one, and puffed dutifully.

"I'll just have to let the news digest, Dad. I can hardly believe it!" he said, very calmly – he couldn't let his true feelings show.

He left the drink and rushed past his father, through the little conservatory, out to the garden. His pre-fab studio stood on the other side of the town. Bush ran across to it and shut himself in.

She was dead... No, she couldn't be, not while there was still so much unfinished between them! If he'd come back punctually... But she was all right when he left. He just had not imagined she, his mother, could die. God, he'd change the damned natural laws if he could!

He raised his fist, shook it, ground his teeth. There had been too many shocks to his ego. Dazedly, he glared about, fixing his gaze with loathing on the Goya, "Chronos Devouring His Children". A reproduction of Turner's "Rain, Steam and Speed" hung on another wall; that too, with its terrifying threat of dissolution, was unbearable. On a shelf stood one of Takis' electric sculptures, dating from the nineteen-sixties, dulled with dust, broken, a ruin that no longer illuminated. Worse were Bush's own attempts at expression, his canvases, sketches, montages, plastic websculptures, groupages, the last SKGs he had done. All were meaningless now, a progression without progress.

Bush set about wrecking the studio, flailing his arms, hardly aware of his hoarse cries and sobs. The whole place seemed to fly apart.

When he came back to consciousness, he was lying back in the dentist's chair. His father was sitting nearby, still abstractedly drinking whisky.

"How did I get here?"

"Are you okay now?"

"How did I get here?"

"You walked. Then you seemed to pass out. I hope it wasn't the whisky."

Bush could not answer that foolishness. His father had never understood him; there was nobody to understand now.

Slowly, he pulled himself together.

"How've you managed, Father? Who's looking after you?"

"Mrs Annivale, from next door. She's very good."

"I don't remember Mrs Annivale."

"She moved last year. She's a widow. Husband shot in the revolution."

"Revolution? What revolution?"

His father looked uneasily over his shoulder. Viewed through the conservatory, the neglected garden lay empty in the April sun. Seeing no spies there, his father was encouraged to say, "The country went bankrupt, you know. All this expenditure on mind-travel, and no returns... There were millions of unemployed. The armed forces went over on to their side, and the government was chucked out. It was hell here for a few months! You were best out of the country. I was glad your mother didn't live to see the worst of it."

Bush thought of The Amniote Egg, prospering. "The new government can't stop mind-travel, can it?"

"Too late! Everyone's hooked on it. It's like drink, knits up the ravelled sleave of care and all that. We've got a military government now, runs exports and imports and so on, but the Wenlock Institute has a large share in the government – so they say. I don't take any notice. I don't take any notice of anything any more. They came to me and ordered me to work at the barracks, looking after the soldiers' oral hygiene. I told 'em I've got my practice here. If your soldiers want to, they can come down here to me, but I'm not going up there to them, and you can shoot me before I do! They haven't bothered me again."

"What happened to the cherry trees in the front?"

"Last winter was terrible. Worst one I can ever remember! I had to chop them down for firewood. Just out of pity, I had Mrs Annivale in here to live with me. She had no heating. Purely altruistic, Ted, I prefer the bottle to sex these days, like a baby. I'm an old man, you know, seventy-two last birthday. Besides, I'm faithful to the memory of your mother."

"I'm sure you miss her very much."

"You know what Shelley said, 'When the lute is broken, Sweet tones are remembered not; when the lips have spoken, Loved accents are soon forgot.' All nonsense! Many things you take no notice of till they're long past, many actions you don't even understand until years after they are performed. By golly, your mother could be a bitch to me at times. She made me suffer! You don't know!"

Bush admitted nothing.

His father continued without pause, as if following a rational train of thought. "And one afternoon when the times were at their worst, the troops were rioting through the city. They burnt down most of Neasden. Mrs Annivale came in here for protection: she was crying. Two soldiers caught a girl up the road. I didn't know her name – the people have changed so much here in these last few years – I don't keep up with them any more – either they've got marvellous teeth or jaws full of rotten ones, because they don't bother me much. Anyhow, she was a pretty girl, only about twenty, and one of these soldiers dragged her up here, into the front garden – my front garden! – and got her down by the wall. It was a nice summer day and the trees were still there then. He was terribly brutal! She struggled so, you see. He practically tore every shred of clothes off her. Mrs Annivale and I watched it all from the waiting-room window."

His eyes were glowing; there seemed to be new life in him. Bush wondered what had passed between Mrs Annivale and him on that occasion.

Here were the images of violence and hate again, from which he was never free. What had this rape to do with his father's recollections of his mother? Was it all a fantasy his father had invented to express his lusts, his aggressiveness, his hatred of women, his fear? It was all a puzzle he never wanted to solve; nor was the ancient tabu against talking sex with his father resolved just because his father was already drunk; but he saw that perhaps he had not been the only person to have been shut out from his mother's love. He wanted to hear nothing more, longed for the claustrophobic silences of the long past.

When he got up, his father recollected himself.

"Men are like animals," he said. "Bloody animals!"

Once there had been a tabu against arguing with his father. That at least had died where the lobe fins crawled, or some dim place where he had been in retreat from his own life.

"I never heard of an animal committing rape, Father. That's man's prerogative! Reproduction was a neutral act, like eating or sleeping or peeing, when it was left to the animals. But in man's hands he's twisted it to mean anything he wants – an instrument of love, an instrument of hate..."

His father drained his glass, set it down and said coldly, "You are afraid of it, aren't you? Sex, I mean. You always were, weren't you?"

"Not at all. You're projecting your fears on to me. But would it be strange if I was, considering the way you used to scoff at me as a kid whenever I brought a girl home?"

"Good old Ted, never forget a grudge, just like your mother!"

"And you must have been pretty afraid of it too, eh, or wouldn't you have chanced your arm and given me some brothers and sisters?"

"You should have asked your mother about that side of things."

"Ha! Those loved accents are not soon forgot, are they? Christ, what a trio we are!"

"Twosome – only you and me now, and you'll have to be patient with me."

"No, a trio still! It takes more than death to get rid of memories, doesn't it?"

"Memories are all I possess now, son – I'm no mind-traveller, able to live in the past... I've just got another bottle upstairs, just for emergencies." James Bush rose and shuffled out of the room. His son followed helplessly. They went up through the dark at the top of the stairs into the tiny sitting-room, which smelt rather damp.

The dentist switched on the electric fire. "We've got a hole in the roof. Don't touch the ceiling or the plaster may come down.

It'll dry off in the summer, and I'll try and fix it. Things are very difficult. Perhaps you'll lend a hand if you're still around."

He brought out a whole bottle of whisky, more than three-quarters full. They had carried their glasses upstairs with them. They sat down on mouldering chairs and grinned at each other. James Bush winked. "To the ruddy old human race!" he said. "A man's a man for a' that!" They drank up.

"We're ruled by a man called General Peregrine Bolt. It seems he's not a bad man as dictators go. Got a lot of popular support. At least he keeps the streets quiet at night."

"No more rapes?"

"Don't let's start on that again."

"What has Bolt done to the Institute?"

"It's prospering, by all accounts. Of course, I know nothing. It's nothing to do with me. It's run on more military lines, I hear."

"I ought to report. I'll go first thing tomorrow, or they'll sack me."

"You're not going back into the past again? The new government will organize all that. Now there are so many people mind-travelling, crime rates are rising back there. Two fellows got murdered in the Permian last week, so the grocer told Mrs Annivale. General Bolt has set up a Mind-Travel Police Patrol to keep order."

"It's orderly enough. I didn't see any crime. A few thousand people spread over millions of years – what harm can it do?"

"People don't stay spread, do they? Still, if you are bent on going back, I can't stop you. Why don't you settle down here and do some groupages and that, make some real money? Your stuff's all in the studio. You can live here."

Bush shook his head. He couldn't talk about his work. The drink was making his neck throb again. His ear ached. Perhaps what he most wanted was a good sleep. At least he could do that here; there seemed to be few invasions of his father's privacy.

Just as he settled his glass down on the wide arm of his chair, there was a thunderous knocking at the front door.

"It says 'Ring and Walk In' clearly enough, doesn't it?"

But his father had gone pale. "That's no patient. It's probably the military. We'd better go and see. Ted, you come down too, won't you? It may be for you. I haven't done anything. I'll just hide this bottle under the chair. They're getting very anti-black market, damn them! What can they want? I've done nothing. I hardly ever go out…"

Muttering, he went downstairs with Bush close behind him. The peremptory hammering came again before they were down. Bush pushed past his father into the waiting-room and went and flung the front door open.

Two armed men in uniform stood on the step. They wore steel helmets and looked far from peaceful. A truck waited behind them in the street, its engine running noisily.

"Edward Lonsdale Bush?"

"That's me. What do you want?"

"Failure to report to Wenlock Institute after overstaying term of mind-travel. You're in trouble and you'll have to come along with us."

"Look, Sergeant, I'm on my way to the Institute now!"

"Short cut, is it? You've been boozing – smell it a yard off! Come on!"

He reached back and grabbed his pack off the magazine-strewn table.

"My notes are all here, I tell you, I'm on my way – "

"No arguing, or we'll charge you with riot and you'll find yourself looking at the wrong end of a firing squad. Quick march!"

He looked round despairingly, but his father had shrunk back into the gloom and was not to be seen. They ushered Bush down the path, past the crumbling brick wall where the rape had been committed, hustled him into the waiting truck, shut the door on him. The truck moved away.

chapter five

a new man at the institute

He found it odd that on the journey he did not waste his time in tension but instead thought lovingly of his father. The old boy had his back against the wall, was to be pitied. His days of dubious power were over; now the situation was reversed – or would be if Bush ever got back to that dingy little house.

Although family grievances were irreparable, that very fact meant that there were unaccountable lulls between the storms, lulls full of the best peace of all, the peace of indifference, when all the horrid things had been said. That was like the incest theme which was popularly supposed to underlie all family quarrels: a mixture of the forbidden best and sweetest and the worst.

He started to think about his mother's death then, testing his reactions. He was still at it when the truck drew to a violent halt and he slid along the bench and landed with a smack against the rear doors. They were flung open, and he half tumbled out.

While his hands were still on the ground, before he had straightened up between his captors, he took in the dreary surroundings behind the truck. They had driven through a barrier, now closing again, set in a high concrete wall. There were guards rigid at the gate and lounging at a couple of shacks that stood under the wall. The grounds as if recently cleared, were littered with rubble.

The two soldiers led him round past the truck and towards an entrance in a large but unimposing building. With disbelief, Bush recognized it as the Wenlock Institute.

The confusion latent in anyone's mind who has moved between different times and experienced yesterday as tomorrow and tomorrow as yesterday sprang up and overwhelmed him. For a while, he could not believe he was in the right year. The Institute had stood in a quiet side street, with a car park on one side of it, and buildings on the other side and opposite it; it had faced across to an insurance office which had done good business with mind-travellers.

He was marched into the Institute before he had the simple answer. Under the régime of the worthy General Peregrine Bolt, the Institute had been advanced in status; his father had told him that. They had merely demolished the rest of the street and built a wall about the premises, so that the Institute could now be easily defended and everyone who entered or left could be accounted for.

Inside, the Institute had changed very little. Indeed, it seemed to have entered on a period of prosperity; the lighting was better, the flooring improved; closed circuit television had been installed, its bowls transmitting coloured messages steadily. The reception desk had been greatly extended – there were now four uniformed men behind it. The boredom and unease generated by their uniform did more to transform the once unpretentious atmosphere than all the other alterations.

The guards presented a scrap of paper. A uniformed receptionist talked into a silenced phone. They all waited. Finally, the receptionist nodded, hung up, and said "Room Three". The guards marched Bush over to Room Three – a cubicle on the main corridor – and left him.

The room was empty except for two chairs. Bush stood in the middle of the room, clutching his pack, listening. It seemed as if he had got off lightly; all the horrors he had had in mind, the punches in the teeth, the kicks in the testicles, those characteristic gestures of a totalitarian régime, receded a little. Perhaps his captors had merely had orders to deliver him here as speedily as possible to make his report. He hoped Howells was still here; Howells always took his report and – Bush had recognized the symptoms long ago – secretly admired and envied him.

Anxiety made him breathe fast and shallowly. The room was like a little box, and they were keeping him waiting a suspiciously long time.

He would be in trouble. If only they would not mention the year he had overstayed – if they could understand he had meant to come back, to work properly, to report. He was their star minder.

Or – his brain ran along another track – if it wasn't old Howells but a new man, who did not know he had overstayed his allotted period. But a new man…a totalitarian…one of Bolt's men…

Knowing absolutely nothing about the current political situation beyond the few words his father had dropped, Bush began to weave a terrible plot in his head, in which he was subject to brutality and in his turn inflicted humiliation on others. It was as if, with the passing of his mother, his mind had to find other complications to stuff itself with. Recent events, the brush with Lenny's gang, the unexpected blow from Stein, the shock of finding how Borrow had so effortlessly achieved what he hoped to do, the news that his mother was dead for some months, were too much for him. He feared he could endure nothing more.

Sinking back on to a corner chair, Bush took his head in his hands and let the universe thump and rock about him.

Indescribable things rushed through him. As though galvanised by a shock, he jumped up rigid. The flimsy door was open and a messenger stood there. Something was the matter with Bush's eyes; he could not make the man out clearly.

"Do you want me to make my report now?" Bush asked, jumping forward.

"Yes, if you'll follow me."

They took the elevator up to the second floor, where Bush usually went to report. A macabre terror gripped him, a premonition of great ill. It seemed to him that the very interior of the Institute had altered in some way, its perspectives and shadows grown more inhuman, its elevators more cruel, while the metal grill of the elevator closed over Bush like fangs. He was sweating when he leapt out into the upper corridor.

"Am I seeing Reggie Howells?"

"Howells? Who's Howells? He doesn't work here any more. I've never heard of him."

The report room looked as he recalled it, except for the telebowl and one or two additional installations which gave it a sly and watchful atmosphere. There were chairs on either side of the table, report pads, the speech/picture humming idly in one corner. Bush was still standing there, clenching and unclenching his fists, when Franklin entered.

Franklin had been Howells' deputy; he was a porky, pale man with goosey flesh and poor eyesight. His eyes swam behind little steel-rimmed glasses. Not at all prepossessing, and Bush recalled now that he had never much liked the man or tried to ingratiate himself with him. He greeted him rather effusively now – it was an unexpected relief to see anyone he knew, even Franklin. Franklin looked puffier, bigger – a foot taller.

"Sit down and make yourself comfortable, Mr. Bush. Put your pack down."

"I'm sorry I didn't report at once, but my mother – "

"Yes. The Institute is being run more efficiently than when you were last here. In future, you will report here *directly* you return to the present. As long as you obey the rules you can come to no harm. Get it?"

"Yes, quite, I see. I'll remember. I hear Reggie Howells has left. So the messenger was telling me."

Franklin looked at him and closed his eyes slightly. "Howells was shot, to tell you the truth."

Bush could not exactly say why, but it was the phrase "to tell you the truth" that upset him; it was too colloquial to follow the content of the rest of the sentence. He decided it might be safer not to say anything more on the subject of Howells; at the same time, he concluded that the most ill-advised thing he could possibly do would be what he most desired: to bust Franklin one on his piggy nose.

To hide his confusion, he put his shabby old pack on the table and started to unzip it.

"I'll open that," Franklin said, pulling the pack towards him. He pushed it under a machine by his right hand, looked at a panel above it, grunted, and ripped it open, tipping its contents out between them. Together, they eyed the poor bric-à-brac that had accompanied Bush over such a great span of time.

Chilled by apprehension, Bush felt his bowels contract. His time sense was awry, too, as it had been when Stein hit him. Franklin was reaching out towards the rubbish on the table, his arm moving perfectly under control, a multi-dimensional figure for a series of intricate reactions between nervous and muscular systems and terrestrial gravitational forces, in which air pressure and optical judgements were also involved. It was a textbook case of anatomical mechanics; as Bush watched it, he could see the crude substructure of the gesture. As the humerus swung slightly forward, ulna and radius levered from it, wrist bent, finger bones extended like the maimed wings of a bird; under the blue serge sleeve, lymph chugged.

Disgusted, Bush looked up at the man. The little astigmatic eyes were still staring at him, isolated behind their glasses, but the face was a bare diagrammatic example of a skull, part of the flesh cut away to reveal teeth, palate, and the intricacies of the inner ear. A series of small red arrows sprayed from the gaping jaws into the air towards Bush, indicating the passage of the organism's breath as it said, "Family Group".

It was reading from a sheet of paper it had retrieved from the debris on the table. The paper had been screwed up. The organism had flattened it out and was examining it.

The paper bore a crude sketch in colour, showing a deserted landscape with a metal sea; from a sun, from a tree, faces protruded. Slowly, Bush realized it was something he had executed in the Devonian; he had scrawled on it the title the organism had read out.

He closed his eyes and moved his head from side to side. When he looked again, Franklin appeared normal once more, his anatomy decently covered by his suit. He had crumpled up the drawing again and thrown it aside in disgust. Now he was examining more sketches, a series Bush had made on a pad. These sketches were of cryptic forms that never entirely transmuted into any recognizable shape. Bush had piled them up on the page, trying to make them ungraspable, defying unidirectional sense, violating all durations.

"What are these?" Franklin asked.

Perhaps I will just clear my throat, Bush thought. He experienced a certain tension there. This was all very unpleasant. No point, of course, in explaining... He cleared his throat, enjoyed some relief as the mucus ceased its tiny pressure. It was erroneous to assume that events in space-time could be rendered by symbols on to paper – a cardinal error that had stood mankind in good stead ever since the first cave paintings. Perhaps you could invent a way to translate into space-time. But that was constantly done. A piece of music...

"My notebooks..."

Nodding, Franklin accepted this as an adequate answer. He put the pad carefully on a side tray, a deliberate gesture. For a moment, he threatened to dissolve into a motor-energy diagram, and Bush fought the feeling back.

"I – my notebooks..."

The illusion, whatever it was, was over. Time snapped back to normal. He could smell the dull atmosphere of the room again, hear noises, the slight sound of Franklin scuffling about in his equipment.

Franklin picked out the notebooks and the wrist camera, sweeping the rest of the stuff into a side tray, a woman's photograph among it.

"Your personal possessions will be returned to you later."

He clipped the first book into the miniscanner on the wall and let it run. Bush's taped voice filled the room, and the recorder behind Franklin redigested it.

Franklin sat where he was without expression, listening.

Bush began to drum with his fingers on the table, then pulled them onto his knees. The books took twenty-five minutes each to play and there were four and a half of them full of his reports, spaced over his long months away. When one book was emptied, Franklin inserted the next without comment. He had been trained to make people uneasy; two or three years ago, he would have coughed and twitched in the unpleasant atmosphere, now Bush did it for him.

The reports had been designed for Howells' ears, genial Howells who welcomed any chit-chat. They contained little new information about the past, although there was a reassuringly solid bit on the phragmoceras, and Bush had genuinely researched into the length of earlier years, which increased the farther one progressed back in time, through the decreased effect of the moon's breaking effect on the Earth by tidal friction. He had confirmed that in the early Cambrian Period, a year consisted of about 428 days. He had also carefully noted the psychological effects of CSD and mind-travel. But too much of the report now seemed like idle chatter about the people he had met on his wanderings through time, interspersed with artistic notes. When the last book drew to its end, after almost two hours of playback, he could hardly bring himself to look at Franklin, who seemed to have been expanding all this time, as Bush himself was shrinking.

Franklin spoke mildly enough. "What would you conceive the objectives of this Institute to be, Bush?"

"Well... It began as a research centre for mental analysis, enlarging the discovery of the undermind – the theory of it. I'm not scientifically trained, I'm afraid I can't phrase it too precisely. But Anthony Wenlock and his researchers discovered the uses of CSD and opened up the new avenues of the mind that have enabled us to overcome the barriers our ancient ancestors put up to protect themselves from space-time, and so mind-travel was developed. That's simplified. I mean, I understand there are still paradoxes to be unravelled, but... Well, anyhow, now the Institute is the HQ of mind-travel, devoted to a greater scientific understanding of...well, of the past. As I say, I – "

"How would you say you served that 'devotion to a greater scientific understanding', as you put it?"

The recorder was still growling away, holding on for posterity to the insincerity in his voice. He knew he was being trapped. Making an effort he said, "I've never pretended to be a scientist. I'm an artist. Dr Wenlock himself interviewed me. He believed artistic insights were needed as well as strictly – well, scientific ones. Also, they found that I was a particularly good subject for mind-travel. I can go farther and faster than most travellers, and get closer to the present. You know all this. It's on my cards."

"But how would you say you serve the 'devotion to greater scientific understanding' you talk so much about?"

"I suppose *you* think not very well. I've said, I'm not a scientist. I'm more interested – well, I've done my best but I'm more interested in people. Damn it, I've done the job I was paid for. In fact, there's quite a bit of back-pay owing."

Franklin blinked somewhat, as if it were a hobby he was taking up. "I'd say by the evidence of these reports of yours that you had almost utterly neglected the scientific side of things. You wasted your time skylarking about. You didn't even stick to the era you were consigned to."

Privately, Bush felt the truth of what Franklin said. This — perhaps fortunately — prevented him from saying anything. He cleared his throat instead; the fist in the teeth, the boot in the testicles, were advancing again.

"On the other hand, you pick up a lot of stuff about people."

Bush nodded. He had spotted that Franklin did not care much for his failure to reply, and felt a little better.

Franklin leaned across the desk and pointed a finger at Bush's face as if suddenly detecting something strange in the room. "The objectives of this Institute have changed since your day, Bush. You're out of date — we have more important things to worry about now than your 'greater scientific understanding'. You'd better get that idea out of your mind. But it was never in very firm, was it? Well, we're on your side now."

He watched to see the effect this reprieve had on Bush, a sneer on his face. Bush hung his head, disgraced to find such base support for his betrayal of science. Regarding himself as an artist, he had loftily thought of himself as in some measure opposed to science, a supporter of the particular against the general; he saw suddenly how faint, how wishy-washy the notion was; his sort of nonsense had helped this other sort of opposition to science, which he recognized — perhaps from the very smell of this bullying room — as altogether antithetical to human values. He'd gone badly wrong if Franklin could say, even as a sour joke, that they were both on the same side.

His courage came back. He got up. "You're right. I'm out of date! I'm a flop! Okay, I resign from the Institute. I'll hand in my notice right away."

The other man permitted himself one blink. "Sit down, Bush, I haven't finished yet. You *are* out of date as you say. Under the present system of employment, and for the duration of the emergency — I suppose you have grasped there *is* an emergency? — no man can leave his job."

"*I* could leave. I'd just refuse to mind-travel!"

"Then you would be imprisoned, or perhaps worse. Sit down, or shall I call some of our new staff? Better! Look, Bush, I'll give it you straight – the economy is being wrecked because people are all mind-travelling, going by the thousands, the hundreds of thousands! They're getting hold of bootleg CSD; it comes in from abroad. They're disaffected elements, and they represent a threat to the régime – to you and me, Bush. We want men to go back there in mind and check on what's happening, trained men. You'd do a good job there with your talents – and it is a good job – well paid, too – the general sees to that. A month's intensive training, and we are going to send you back with proper status, provided you're sensible."

Trying to sort through what the man said, Bush asked, "Sensible? How do you mean, sensible?"

"Useful. A functioning part of the community. You've got to give up this idea of chasing your own personality down the ages."

When he had let that sink in, Franklin added, "Forget all that business about wanting to be an artist. That's all finished, washed up! There's no market or opportunity for works of art any more, and anyhow, you've lost the knack now, haven't you? Borrow proved that to you, surely!"

Bush bowed his head. Then he forced his eyes to meet the slippery ones behind the little lenses watching him from the other side of the table.

"Okay," he managed to say. It was a complete submission to Franklin's argument, an acceptance of everything he had said, an admission that he was useless in any role but that of spy or snoop or informer, or whatever they would call it: but even as he delivered himself over to what he recognized instinctively as the enemy, he was born anew in courage and determination, for he saw that his one chance as an artist was to move again as a mind-traveller – saw, moreover, that he was less an artist than a mind-traveller, the first of a new breed whose entire *métier* was mind-travel, that he would rather die than lose this weird liberty of the mind; and as a corollary to that discovery, he saw that by understanding his personality on this new basis he might eventually come to deliver a new form of art expressing the changed world-view, the new and schizophrenic *zeitgeist*.

Just momentarily, as he glared at Franklin, great joy broke upon Bush; he saw he still had the chance to speak to the world (or the few) of his vision, his unique vision; and then he thought how insignificant he would make the mock-ups of Roger Borrow look; and by that petty step, he came back to reality, and the hum of the recorder, and Franklin's nose and spectacles.

It was Franklin's turn to rise. "If you wait downstairs, they will bring your personal belongings down to you."

"And my pay?"

"*And* your pay. Some of it. The rest will be issued as post-emergency credits. You can go home then. The next course starts Monday; you're on leave till then – don't do anything silly, of course. A truck will pick you up Monday morning early. Be ready! Understood?"

Malice made Bush say, "Well, it's been nice seeing you again Franklin. And what does Dr Wenlock think of all the changes?"

Franklin gave one of his blinks. "You've been away too long, Bush. Wenlock went out of his mind some while ago. To tell you the truth, he's in a mental institution."

chapter six

the clock analogy

It was beginning to rain as he walked past the carious tree stumps and the wall by which rapist and raped had lain together; he climbed the steps to find his father had locked the door. Only after much ringing and knocking and shouting through the letter-box did he persuade his father to come down and open up.

His father had absorbed most of the rest of the whisky. With Bush's back pay, they bought more that evening, and were drunk that night and the next day. The drunkenness was a reliable substitute for the friendship they could not quite establish. It also helped to blot out the terror in Bush's mind.

On the next day, the Thursday, James Bush took his son to inspect his mother's grave. They were both sober and heavy then, needing a dose of melancholy. The cemetery was ancient and abandoned, pitched on such a steep and windy hill that grass would grow only on one side of the mound. It seemed an uncharacteristic place for Elizabeth Lavinia, Beloved Wife of James Bush, to lie. Bush wondered for the first time how she had felt indoors that long day when he was locked out in the garden. Now she was locked out for good, her soul cast on to a steeper, longer beach than any known to Earth's history.

"Her parents were Catholic. She gave up all belief at the age of six."

Six? It seemed a curious time to give up any belief; his father might as well have said "six in the morning".

"Something happened to her when she was six that convinced her there was no God. She'd never tell me what it was."

Bush said nothing. His father had kept off the subject of religion since he had returned from the interview with Franklin. Now he teetered on the brink again; the moment was abominably favourable. Bush began to whistle annoyingly under his breath to counteract his father's advantage. Even the thought of religion irritated him.

He did not believe the story about his mother's loss of faith, or whatever it had been, at the age of six. Had such an event occurred, he would often have heard about it from both his parents, who were not ones to tuck away their woes.

"Better be getting back then, Dad, I suppose." He shuffled his feet. James Bush did not move. He stood looking down at his wife's grave, absently scratching one buttock. Observing him, Bush saw his father put on one of his sanctimonious expressions, which was followed by something perhaps more sincere, perhaps a general empty feeling of puzzlement about what he and Ted and the rest of mankind and the whole writhing bundle of animate things were supposed to be doing with life anyway. Bush found that more alarming than the sanctimonious expression; he was aware enough of where his own enervating self-questioning came from. He hoped his father's years of flirtation with belief were dead and buried; resurrection now would come inconveniently.

"Looks like rain."

"She just didn't know where she stood with God. But she wanted to be buried here. 'Our reasons live their own existences', as the poet Skellet puts it."

"Can we get a bus back?"

"Yes. You'd be surprised – you can't get a headstone for love or money, nowadays. See this one? I made it myself. How do you like it, Ted? Reinforced concrete, and I did the lettering before it was dry."

"Very professional."

"You don't think it should just have been 'E Lavinia'? She never used the Elizabeth."

"It's fine as it is, Dad."

"I was pleased with it."

"Yes."

"Sorry you weren't here for it all. It didn't seem right without you."

So her life ended, not just under that mound where the trickle of water down the hill had already commenced to erode one side of it, but in the exchange of trivialities between her husband and son. As Bush told himself that, he felt convinced that neither of them would come here again. There was a limit to the pointlessness humans could endure.

"But isn't it all bloody pointless?" he said. "Who was she? I don't know, and I doubt whether you do. Was there a point to her life – and if so, what? When she was six? If that tale's true, then the rest of her life was anticlimax, and she'd have done better to live her days backwards, with the cancer healing and her getting young again and eventually gaining her baby faith!"

He checked himself on the verge of terror, and they began to move away from the grave.

His father said, "We didn't ask that sort of question when we got married."

"I'm sorry, Father. Let's go home. I didn't mean what I said – you always had more sense than I did. It's just – "

"You were the point of her life, just as much as me."

"That's all nonsense, unless you believe the whole purpose of the human race is simply to breed another generation and another…"

His father began to walk rapidly downhill, towards the collapsing lych gate.

It was a cold day. The dentist's house felt damp and they lunched poorly on fried potatoes and salt. Food was short and appallingly dear. In the afternoon, Bush read some of the old magazines down in the waiting-room. A patient miraculously appeared, hugging a suppurating gumboil in his jaw, and Bush scowled at the disturbance.

Through the distorting pages of the magazines, he gained a picture of the factors that had gradually brought about the present situation. He had travelled carelessly through life, quarrelling, lovemaking, talking, painting, without any stay to his appetites or reference to the currents that moved through his generation. He saw now that one of the occasional reactions against a high-powered industrial society had set in some years earlier, expressing itself as a fad for the gas-lit glories of the long-dead Victorian Age. Such reactions soon blew over when they had nothing to feed themselves on and a new fad came to distract attention. But in the twenty-seventies, the new thing was mind-travel, or its possibility, which stoked rather than damped the public nostalgia. In a surprisingly short time, certainly by the mid-eighties, the advanced civilizations of the world had reoriented themselves towards the past — the far distant pre-historic past, since that was paradoxically the easiest to reach, the second law of thermodynamics not extending itself to cover the lower reaches of the human mind. A generation grew up which dedicated itself, its energies and abilities, to escaping from their own time. Every human activity was hit, from the tourist trade (Florida's sands, the Mediterranean beaches, were as deserted as in Victorian times) to the steel industry, from entertainment to philosophy.

Amid the brewing of a world slump, only the Wenlock Institutes prospered. There one could enrol for moderately expensive courses to be taught the Wenlock discipline that unlocked the ancient bars of the mind. There one could purchase the drugs that helped one on one's way to the plesiosaur-haunted seas. And at the mind-stations, Wenlock-owned, one could keep a moderately expensive anchorage in the world of passing time while one disappeared – for ever, if the cash held out.

Like other human systems, the Wenlock system, although as humanitarian as its founder, was fallible. In many countries, it was denounced as a dangerous monopoly; in others, it came at once under the direction of the government. And of course, less well-meaning persons ferreted out the secrets of its disciplines and drugs, and put their own versions on the market. Many a refrigerator in many an empty apartment held dishes of blood and tissue cultures, while the absconding family played hookey in Gondwanaland.

Within the Wenlock empire, too, all was not well. An article in *Dental World* for January of the previous year entitled "The Discipline and Dental Pay" first brought the name of Norman Silverstone to Bush's attention, and then he came across it again in one or two of the other tattered magazines. As a commentator pointed out, the whole theory of mind-travel rested on few facts and a mass of supposition, rather as the theories of the psycho-analyst Sigmund Freud had, at the end of the nineteenth and the first half of the twentieth century. Silverstone played Jung to Wenlock's Freud. Although nobody could deny the fact of mind-travel, there were several who denied that Wenlock's was the correct interpretation of it. Most powerful among these was Wenlock's one-time friend and associate, Norman Silverstone. Silverstone maintained that the human mind could certainly be freed from the psychotic barrier behind which it had built its time-locked supremacy over the rest of the animal kingdom; but he claimed that there were yet more extraordinary powers to be released, and that the limitations of mind-travel, debarring most human travellers from most of historic time, was evidence of the fact that the discipline was but a fragment – probably a distorted fragment – of a greater whole.

Silverstone was of a retiring disposition, a man who re-fused to be interviewed or photographed, and his occasional contributions to the dispute were so abstruse that it could hardly be said that he constituted a too formidable opposition to Wenlock. Nevertheless, he and his followers provided an instrument that proved useful to governments wanting to have a hand in the administration of the local institutes and mind-stations.

For obvious reasons, the supply of antique magazines stopped at the time of the revolution, but Bush thought he could see clearly enough the ensuing train of events. In most countries, the severe slump conditions would be accentuated by stock market crashes; unemployed men would march on the capital; the half-starved would riot; tougher governments would be called for, by haves and have-nots alike, although for different reasons. He sat in the untidy room, inventing discomforts.

The unsettled conditions would not last. The nations would recover, as they had recovered before. He already had a sign that General Bolt's régime might be of limited duration – almost a mystical sign, although at the time it had gone nearly unheeded. When he was standing in Room 3, locked in a sort of fit and waiting for the summons before Franklin, the Dark Woman had appeared. At the time, his mind had been too preoccupied for this visitant from the future to register fully with him. But he realized now that shadowy as she was, she had glowed slightly, for all the world like a phantom in the mock Victorian pageants his mother had taken him to as a boy. It could mean only one thing: that, in her age, she was standing in the open; in other words, Institute was demolished in her day; which argued that the General's protective wing would not always be there. Not always, but his phantom watcher might be five hundred years ahead, which was a long time. Well, there was hope. The most dreadful things passed.

He looked round the waiting-room. She was not with him at present. However faithful she was, she had to have some time off duty. Then he thought: Or is she a figment of my imagination, my anima? Aren't I radically unbalanced, by turns cowardly and over-bold, under-sexed and sex-obsessed? Maybe the Dark Woman is just a projection of my dissociated personality.

But she was more than that. She was the future, for its own reasons keeping an eye on him. The future was everywhere in his age, as if they would dam his generation in and repel its angry wave so that the flood of discontent flowed away from it, leaving it Olympian and safe! They had discovered a way of moving among the ages of man.

Bush tried to speculate about the future, gave up, and slipped out of the house for a walk. He could not reason constructively since he had been placed under Franklin's training orders. His life was about to be turned upside down. Indeed, he hardly understood what was going on. In the nights he thought he heard his mother's voice.

He tried to think about Ann, but she seemed as remote as the Devonian in which he had found her. He tried to think about his father, but there was nothing new to think. He thought about Mrs Annivale, whom he had now met, but that made him uncomfortable. Mrs Annivale was not half as horrible as he had pictured her. She was, he judged, no more than his own age and still had something of youth about her. She smiled pleasantly, was friendly and natural, seemed genuinely to like his father, and her mind did not seem too entirely banal. But she was no business of his.

He turned back. There was nowhere he wanted to go to, and the dirty empty streets repelled him. He recalled that in his wrecked studio there was a box of clay he used for modelling; perhaps he could interest himself with that, although every spark of inspiration felt dead.

When the lump he was moulding into shape began to resemble Franklin's head, he gave up and went indoors.

"Had a pleasant day?" Mrs Annivale asked, coming downstairs.

"Just great! We went over to see mother's grave this morning and this afternoon I've had a good read of some two-year-old magazines."

She looked at him and grinned. "You talk quite a bit like your Dad. He's asleep by the way – I shouldn't wake him. I'm just going round to my place to get my grater; I'm going to make you a cheese pud tonight. Why don't you come round with me? You haven't seen my place yet."

Moodily, he went with her. Her house was bright and clean and seemed to contain very little furniture. In the kitchen, Bush asked, "Why don't you move in with father and save rent and everything, Mrs Annivale?"

"Why don't you call me Judy?"

"Because I didn't know it was your name. Father always calls you Mrs Annivale to me."

"Formal! I hope you and I don't have to be formal, do we?" She was standing idly near him, looking at him, showing her teeth a little.

"I asked you why you didn't move in with my father."

"Suppose I said I fancied younger men?" There was no mistaking the tone in her voice or the look in her eye. Everything was convenient, he told himself. Her bed would be clean, his father was asleep next door, she knew he was off next week. Unbidden, his betraying body told him it liked the idea.

Hastily, he turned from her. "Then that's jolly sweet of you to look after him, Judy."

"Look, Ted – "

"Got the cheese grater? We'd better go and see if he's okay." He led the way back, feeling a fool; so evidently did she, judging by the way she chattered. But after all…well, it would have been like incest. There were some things you had to draw the line at, however much of a moral wreck you were!

Although such was not the case, Judy Annivale seemed to imagine she had offended Bush and was tiringly pleasant to him.

Once or twice, he had to take refuge in his studio with the half-formed bust of Franklin. And on the day the truck was due to come for him, she followed him down into the studio.

"Beat it!" he said. He saw death in the lines round her mouth.

"Don't be unsociable, Ted! I wanted to see what you were doing in the art line. I used to think I was artistic once."

"If you want to play with my clay, go ahead, but just don't follow me around! Are you trying to be a mother to me or something?"

"Do you really think I've been showing you signs of motherliness, Ted?"

He shrugged his shoulders. He had no morals. Maybe he was passing up a good opportunity that tomorrow would see lost forever.

James Bush thrust his head inside the shed.

"So this is where you've both got to?"

"I was just saying how much I admired Ted's artistic talents, Jim. I used to be a bit artistic myself once, as a girl. I'm sure all the wide perspectives of the past that you've travelled must have helped a lot."

Perhaps a whisper of suspicion passed over James Bush's brain. In irritation, he said, "Nonsense, the boy's seen next to nothing! You're like most folk – you don't seem to realise how ancient the Earth is and how little of its past is accessible even to mind-travellers."

"Oh, not that clock analogy, Father!" Bush had heard this set-piece before.

But his father was covering the exit. Painstakingly, he explained a standard textbook diagram to Judy, a diagram in which it was supposed that the Earth was created at midnight. Then followed long hours of darkness with no life, the time of fire and an alien atmosphere and long rains, the Pre-Cambrian times or Cryptozoic Era, of which little was known or could be known. The Cambrian period marked the beginning of the fossil record and did not arrive till ten o'clock on the clock face.

The big reptiles and amphibians put in an appearance with the Carboniferous period at about eleven o'clock, and were gone by quarter to twelve. Mankind's appearance was made at twelve seconds to noon, and the time since the Stone age was a fraction of a second.

"That's what I mean about perspectives!" Judy said gamely.

"You perhaps miss the point, my dear. All these grand millions of years the mind-travellers make so free with in their conversation are but the last ten minutes on the dial. Man is a small thing, his little life is not only ended but begun with a sleep."

"The clock analogy is misleading," Bush said. "It doesn't leave room for the immense future, many times all that's past. You think your clock puts everything in perspective but really it ruins it."

"Well, we can't see the future, can we?"

The question was unassailable, at least for a little while.

chapter seven

the squad

The truck delivered Bush at the training centre at 10.30 in the morning. By midday, his civilian clothes had been taken from him, to be replaced by a coarse khaki uniform; his head had been shaved; he had plunged through a cold disinfectant bath; been inoculated against typhoid, cholera, and tetanus, and vaccinated against smallpox; been examined to see that be was not suffering from a venereal disease; had his voice- and retina-patterns taken and his fingerprints recorded; and paraded at the cookhouse for an ill-cooked meal.

The course proper began at 1300 hours sharp, and from then until the end of the month was almost unremitting.

Bush was put in Ten Squad, under a Sergeant Pond. Pond drove his men through a succession of difficult or impossible tasks. They had to learn to march and even to run in step. They had to learn to respond to orders given a quarter of a mile away by the human voice, if such a designation was seemly for Sergeant Pond's noises, shouting at its most ragged and repulsive pitch. They had to learn to climb brick walls and to fall from upper storey windows; they had to learn to swarm up ropes and wade through stagnant pools; they had to learn how to dig meaninglessly deep holes and strangle their fellow men; to shoot and stab and swear and sweat and eat garbage and sleep like dead men. To begin with, a sardonic part of Bush's brain amused itself by standing apart and watching his actions. Now and again, it would come forward and say, "The object of this exercise is to make you less an individual, more a machine for taking orders. If you cross this rope bridge without falling on the rocks below, you will be less human than you were before you attempted it. Gobble down this bit of sea-lion pie and you will be even less of an artist than you were yesterday." But the sardonic part of Bush's brain was soon anaesthetized by constant meaningless activity. He was too tired and bemused for criticism to flourish, and the harsh roar of Pond's voice supplanted the whisper of his intelligence.

Nevertheless, he was alert enough to notice the activities of some of his fellow recruits. Most of them, the great majority, accepted and suffered as he did, putting their private selves away, as it were, the better to endure. There were also two small minorities; one consisted of those unfortunates who could not put away their private selves. They got on parade late with their boots dusty; they could not eat the food; they turned left when the rest turned right; they half-drowned in the scummy ponds; sometimes, they wept instead of sleeping at night.

The other small minority called themselves "The Tripeshop Troopers". They were the ones who enjoyed Sergeant Pond's insults, who relished the degradations of the barrack square, who were born for stabbing sawdust dummies. And in their spare time, they drank wildly, beat up the members of the other minority, vomited unexpectedly on the floor, sucked up to Pond and generally behaved like heroes.

They also gave the squad its backbone and spirit, and Bush wondered afterwards if he would have got through the course without his desire to prove himself as good and tough as they.

He did best, and outshone the rest of the course, only on the firing range, where the squad frittered away every Monday and Thursday morning in draughty surroundings. Here, they learned to fire light-guns, which might (or more probably might not) become standard items of their equipment later. The light-guns fired pulsed beams of coherent light that could burn a neat little black hole right through a man at half a mile. But it was less the killing potentialities of the weapon than its artistic side that attracted Bush. This slender metal barrel dealt with the basic substance of all painters, light: ordered it, organized it; the ruby laser it contained spat out light in milliseconds' worth, delivering it in parallel, monochrome beams onto target. As Bush burned out his bull's-eyes, he felt he was indulging in the only artistic pursuit left to a man in time of emergency.

Among all the marching, chasing, and mock fights to which Ten Squad was subjected, lectures were given on various subjects. The squad then sat on benches in blessed momentary peace, and Bush sometimes snatched these periods to wonder what the object of the course was.

Clearly, it had been cobbled quickly together from other established military courses, but he could not see that it had much connection with his future as an agent which had been mapped out for him. He appreciated that he was being systematically degraded, and perhaps more effectively than the Tripeshop Troopers, who gloatingly took all the punishment meted out. He just failed to see its purpose; and then he realized what all this would mean to the undermind; knowing its own worth, it would be shamed and defeated, and would die more easily when ordered to.

But that was nonsense, because... Their duty was not to die. The hatred Sergeant Pond injected into them for twelve hours a day was to help them suffer, not die. The undermind was being fed poison – and nobody was protesting! They must be mad. And this conspiracy was no freak of General Bolt's régime; it was ubiquitous, eternal. Men had always poisoned themselves in this way, making themselves coarse of habit, dim of wit, void of individuality. As an artist, he had always been alone. Now for the first time, he was surrounded by his fellow men, and he saw into them. They had windows in their chests. There was something moving in there, peering out through the windows;

the windows were misty, steamed over by the breath as it was sucked in among the sponges of the lungs; it was hard to see. One of the things inside was writing on the window with a finger. It was a message for help, something explaining the sanity of all mankind, but not only were the letters back to front, they ran in the wrong direction. Bush was on the verge of deciphering the words when –

His name was called, and he sat up abruptly.

His name was called, and he had been asleep!

"Bush, you have ten seconds to answer the question." A red-faced officer, one Captain Stanhope, stood by the blackboard, glaring at Bush. The rest of the squad had turned round to stare and the Troopers were grinning and nudging each other. "The carotid vein!" one whispered across at Bush.

"The carotid vein, sir," Bush said, clutching at a straw.

The squad rocked with laughter. The Troopers nearly fell on to the floor in their delight.

Stanhope barked for silence. When the squad had been reduced to silence, he said, "All right, Bush, I asked you what carrots were good for. You tried to be funny. I'll deal with you afterwards."

Bush directed a glare of hatred at the hearties.

He marched up to the captain afterwards, as the rest of the squad was clattering out, and stood rigidly at attention till the officer deigned to notice him.

"You were trying to be funny at my expense."

"No, sir. I was asleep."

"Asleep! What do you mean, asleep, when I was talking?"

"I'm exhausted, sir. There's too much running around on this course."

"What were you in pre-revolutionary days?"

"Artist, sir. I did groupages and that sort of thing."

"Oh. What's your name?"

"Bush, sir."

"I know that. Your full name, man."

"Edward Bush."

"Then I know your work." Stanhope softened slightly. "I used to be an architect before the need for architecture disappeared. I admired some of the things you did. Liked your groupages, especially the one you made for Southall station; the spatial-kinetic series you did was a revelation. I have – had – a book on your work, with illustrations."

"The one by Branquier?"

"That's the name, Branquier. Well, I'm happy to meet you, though hardly in these surroundings and conditions. You're an expert mind-traveller, too, I hear."

"I've been doing it a long time."

"You shouldn't be on a course like this! Weren't you picked for minding by Wenlock himself?"

"That may be partly why I'm here."

"Mm. I see. What do you think of this Wenlock–Silverstone controversy? Don't you feel that the Wenlock orthodoxy may well be a myth, and that Silverstone in fact has a great deal to offer if his side of the matter were not distorted? So many suppositions have been taken for facts, haven't they?"

"I don't know, sir. I know nothing about it."

Stanhope smiled. "They've gone now. You can speak freely to me. Quite honestly, the régime are all wrong in hunting Silverstone, aren't they? Don't you think?"

"As I said, sir, it's a tough course. I can't think any more. I have no opinions."

"But as an artist, on a vital matter like Silverstone, you must have very strong opinions."

"No, none sir. Blisters on feet and hands, sir; no opinions."

Stanhope drew himself up. "Bush, dismiss – and next time I catch you dozing in my lectures, you'll be in bad trouble."

Bush marched away, solid and flat-footed. Inwardly, he laughed and sang. The bastards weren't going to catch him that easily!

But he wondered very much about the news that the régime was hunting Silverstone. It sounded authentic. And why should they be sounding out his views on the subject?

At that time, he had only two weeks to run before he found out, but those two weeks dragged on interminably as the course went its pointless way. Being antisocial, Bush found barrack-room life no pleasanter when it became clear that his brush with Stanhope had made him something of a favourite with the Troopers.

"What ho, mate! How's the old carrots going down?" they would call, with oafish good-humour, never tired of his lewd answer.

At last, the final straw dummy had been stabbed, the last illiterate talk on seeing without being seen listened to, the last mile run. Ten Squad paraded for its final tests, followed by personal interviews, alone in the shabby lecture huts with two officers.

Bush found himself with a bald-headed man, Captain Howes, and Captain Stanhope.

"You can sit down," Stanhope said. "We are going to ask you a series of questions, just to test your knowledge and reaction speed. What is wrong with this sentence: 'Nature and nature's laws lay hid in night. God said let Newton be and all was light'?"

"It's an accurate quote from some poet or other – Pope? But it isn't true. There's no God, and Newton didn't illuminate as much as his generation supposed."

"What's wrong with this sentence: 'The régime are mistaken in persecuting Silverstone'?"

"Collective noun should be followed by singular verb."

Stanhope scowled. "What else?"

"I don't know."

"Why not?"

"What régime? What Silverstone? I don't know."

"Next question." They went on through a maze of trivia, the captains taking it in turn to interrogate, sitting staring moodily at Bush while they were resting. At last the farce came to an end.

Captain Howes cleared his throat and said, "Cadet Edward Bush, we are pleased to say that you have passed your test. We allot you a score of about eighty-nine per cent, with the rider that you have an unstable personality, peculiarly suited to mind-travel. We hope to send you on a special mission into the past within a few days."

"What sort of a mission?"

Howes laughed unconvincingly. He was a big man, not ill-looking, who seemed more in control than Stanhope. "Come, you've had enough for today! Relax, Bush! The course is over. Captain Stanhope and I will see you back here tomorrow morning at nine-thirty, to give you full briefing. Till then, you can go away and celebrate."

He bent down and pulled a bottle out of the drawer of the desk, handing it solemnly over to Bush. "Don't imagine the régime has no time for fun, Bush, or no sense of the better things in life. Go and enjoy yourself and accept this gift with the compliments of the officers of the course."

When they had gone, Bush examined the bottle of drink with some curiosity. It had a big tartan label and was called "Black Wombat Special: Genuine South Indian Rice Whisky, Brewed in Madras from a Forbidden Recipe". He flipped up the metal cap and sniffed cautiously. He shivered.

Tucking the bottle inside his tunic, he took it back to the barrack-room.

The Tripeshop Troopers were already celebrating the end of the course, drinking vile resinous drinks out of tiny mugs. They greeted Bush with a cheer and arch references to the carotid vein. Destined to begin life anew as members of the newly formed mind-travel police, working in mufti, they had a week's leave coming to them on the morrow. They were vowing to spend the whole leave drunk.

Bush presented them with the Forbidden Recipe Whisky. As he sat down with them, he found Sergeant Pond was among them, Pond whose kindest words in the last month had been to damn them for a ruddy herd of ruptured bleeding camels, Pond who bayed at them like a bloodhound and worried them like a terrier.

Pond put his arm about Bush. "You been my besh squad, you boys! What'm I going to do without you? Another ruddy shower of recruits in tomorrow, needing their noshesh wiped all the time. You're my frien's!"

Gritting his teeth, Bush poured some Forbidden Recipe on top of the brown liquid already in Pond's mug.

"Yer my besh frien', Bush," the sergeant said. His maltreated voice, grinding along in low gear, could hardly be heard for the band now starting up, as some of the brighter or more stupid lads began to whistle and shout and sing and beat a crude rhythm out on waste bins, mess tins, and other instruments. Bracing himself, Bush took a swig at the Black Wombat, and was instantly three parts drunk.

Four hours later, almost every man in the barrack-room was in a sodden stupor. Pond had staggered away into the night, the squaddies had either fallen into bed or been thrown there by hearty companions. One man stood alone at the far end of the room by a window flung wide, still clutching a bottle, and singing a lewd song.

> *"...But the way he caught the butler*
> *Was the dirtiest way of all..."*

Finally there were silence and darkness. Bush lay on his bed, wakeful under a feeling of terror that had an illusive familiarity about it.

"I'm not dying, am I?" he whispered. He could hear voices. There seemed to be four men round his bed, two in white coats, two in black. One of them said, "He can't understand a thing you say; it's all turned to his own needs. He imagines himself in another place, perhaps another time. Isn't he a committed insect?"

The thought of insects goaded Bush into sitting upright. The gaunt bleak room full of insensible bodies stretched away in all directions. The four men still stood at his bedside. Humouring his fantasy, he said, "Where do you felons think I am?"

"Quietly!" one of the phantoms admonished. "You'll wake the others in the wardrobe. You're suffering from anoxia, with ordinary hallucinations."

"But the window's open," he protested. "Where is this, anyway?"

"The Garfield Mental Hospital. We are looking after you; we believe you are an amniote egg."

"Your meeting's scrambled," he said. He sank down again, overwhelmed by sensations of drunkenness and futility. These men could do nothing for him or to him. On his pillow, a yawning pit of sleep awaited him.

He made it to the lecture hut on time next morning, despite a throbbing head. Howes and Stanhope arrived in a few minutes. They were in civilian clothes. The course was over – until the next one began. In the square, the disbanded Ten Squad were moving about in unfamiliar clothes, heading away from home or duty, bawling final ribaldries at each other.

The officers sat down on the bench next to Bush, and Stanhope began to talk in a businesslike way.

"We know you will be honoured by the mission the government has in mind for you. However, before we tell you what it is, we feel it necessary to give you some of the wider background.

"This is a time of great uncertainty, nationally and internationally, as you are by now aware. The new theory of time has upset the status quo. This is particularly so in the West – America and Europe, which have for historic reasons always been the very time-conscious areas. In the East, things are much as they ever were. Duration means a different thing to a Chinaman or Indian than it does to us.

"General Peregrine Bolt had to step in and take over because this country of ours was on the brink of economic ruin. A strong hand is going to be needed for a long while, until we adjust to the new conditions – meanwhile, we are in the paradoxical position of having to accept aid from the East."

Bush's aching head prompted him to say, "Hence the Black Wombat Special, I suppose."

He observed that Stanhope looked blank, whereas Howes caught the reference.

"You will see that it is imperative that no new disruptions come along to upset the order we are trying to build."

"What sort of disruptions do you mean?"

Stanhope looked embarrassed. Howes said, "Ideas are sometimes worse than armed uprisings. As an intellectual, you should know that."

"I'm not an intellectual."

"I'm sorry. Suppose a conflicting idea should now arise about the nature of time? It might throw us back to where we were a few months ago."

Understanding began to creep over Bush. These two men seemed so harmless, so *marginal* (and Stanhope was really not particularly bright); but they were sitting here like two evil uncles at a sick child's bedside, telling him bad fairy stories that might reveal the whole secret of...of the régime's, and consequently Bolt's, fears; of the neuroses of the age... It was something in Howes' face that prompted this feeling; he was being as frank as he dared, he was also hiding something: the classic dilemma of an intelligent man in a totalitarian society.

Howes told Bush, "It's the question of time, you see. All that man is, all that he has built – although, as Captain Stanhope says, this is more true of the West than the East – has been founded on the idea that time is unidirectional: like the flow of water through a sluice gate, shall we say? But this was man's invented idea, and the little he knew of the truth he kept suppressed down in the dark basements of his being, the undermind, as we call it. Occasionally, intimations of the truth have leaked though, to frighten him. Precognitive experiences or dreams, extra-sensory perceptions, the sense of *déjà vu*, and so on – almost anything that could ever be dismissed as magical or superstitious – were such leakages, and directly contradicted the precious theory of unidirectional time. Which was why they were so passionately laughed out of court."

"And your alternative to unidirectional time?"

"Co-continuous time. You know that. You believe it. You went through the Wenlock Discipline. Space-time being what it is, past and present are at par in terms of energy. Imagine a featureless world without day or night or organic processes: we'd have no basis there for any concept of time, even an incorrect one like unidirectionalism, because there would be no way of establishing time differences from a human point of view. The error, the very concept of timeflow, is in the human consciousness, not in the external universe: the creed that causes us to speak of mind-travel rather than time-travel, as some would originally have preferred. Such is Wenlock's discovery and it gives us something to work on. Any other rival theories must be squashed, in case they throw us back into chaos again."

"And I take it there are rival theories?"

He knew what was coming even before Stanhope answered (this was Stanhope's domain, the world of security, so much simpler than the realm of speculation): "You know there are rival theories. The renegade Silverstone, once a colleague of Wenlock's, is uttering dangerous and misleading nonsense."

"Heresy, eh?"

"Don't joke, Bush. Not heresy but treason. Silverstone is guilty of treason by uttering ideas calculated to upset the security of the State. He must be eliminated."

Bush guessed what came next. The madmen who visited him in the night could have guessed. By the very nature of his thinking, Silverstone would be an accomplished mind-traveller. The régime would require another such to go and eradicate him – and Bush was another such.

Howes must have read Bush's expression, for he said, "That is your mission, Bush, and I hope you prove worthy of the honour. You have to hunt down Silverstone and kill him. We know he is somewhere at large in time, probably under an assumed name; we shall give you every assistance."

Snapping open the case he was nursing, he produced a bulky file and held it out to Bush.

"You are going to be given forty-eight hours' leave and then you will be equipped and required to mind-travel until you find the traitor Silverstone. We shall see that your father is provided for; he will appreciate the Black Wombat. You will study these documents and make yourself familiar with Silverstone's case in every way possible...except that of inflicting on yourself the man's treasonable theories."

Catching an edge of irony in Howes' voice, Bush glanced up, but the officer stared at him blank-faced, and Bush dropped his gaze to the dossier. On the top of it lay a photograph of Silverstone, one of the rare ones. It showed a man with long straggly white hair and an untidy grey moustache. His nose was long and curved. Although his eyes in the photo were serious and abstracted, a half-smile lurked about the lips. When Bush had last seen him, his hair had been cut and dyed and his moustache shaved off; but he had no difficult in recognizing Stein.

"I'll see what I can do, gentlemen," he said, "I shall enjoy the assignment."

The captains rose and shook his hand.

chapter eight

a word from william wordsworth

A battered truck drove Bush from the barracks and deposited him at his father's house. Besides his kit, he carried half a case of Black Wombat Special, a present from a grateful government.

He stood on the pavement, watching the truck out of sight. Spring had sunk into dusty summer. The truck seemed hardly able to chug up the road for dust. If the municipal services did not get organized again, the whole road would eventually silt up. Grass and thistles were growing along the gutters. In the dentist's garden, the cherry tree stumps were hidden by a riot of cow parsley and nettles, like tokens of unidirectional change.

Bush stood and sampled what it felt like to be away from the horrible life of Ten Squad. It was rather like escaping from a straitjacket. He could not enter the little house just yet; it looked too confining, and he needed time to breathe. He needed time to breathe... He stood and laughed, thinking of a mobile he could construct, with glittering metal shards representing minutes and seconds being pumped through a pair of bird cages. It would be a small thing to work on until his gift came back.

Hiding the case of whisky among the cow parsley, he began to walk down the road in the direction the truck had taken. No one was about. The scene was colourless. He thought about sex. He tried to remember Mrs Annivale and Ann, but could hardly conjure up their faces. Over the last month, he had been so hard-driven that all sexual urges had left him; even the vision of an hospitably crooked leg and thigh had ceased to torment him. The madness of military discipline he had taken as a sign that mankind was sick in some deep way; otherwise, how could the generations have tolerated that stifling of the individual will? Now he was experiencing one reward that came from such harsh monasticism.

He walked in the by-streets, found an old pond at the end of one, marvelled that he could not remember it. He stood staring into its muddy shallows, cluttered with derelict things, drowned boots and wheels and tins.

Voices came from near at hand. A ruined building stood by the pond; the voices seemed to originate there. Bush started listening when he caught the name Bolt.

"We'd better step up the treatment, hadn't we?"

"Before Bolt does!"

"The sooner the better. This afternoon, if we can get the message through; we were only held up for the lack of £ s. d. I'll provide the contact."

They mentioned another name. Treason? Or maybe it was Gleason.

Bush moved cautiously over to the crumbling building and peered through a foggy window. In the murk, two negroes were talking to two white men. He was suddenly extremely frightened of being caught by them. Making his way quietly from the vicinity of the pond, he started running and did not stop until he was panting outside the dentist's. By that time, he was uncertain whether he had actually seen what he thought he had seen, or whether his nerves were not playing him false. He was a little upset by his mother's death, and needed to get away.

Taking up his kit and the case of whisky, he hurried into the house.

James Bush unstoppered a bottle of the Indian whisky, poured some for Mrs Annivale, Bush, and himself, and listened moodily as Bush spoke of the new life of action on which he was about to embark. He had been instructed not to mention Silverstone. He told them he was going to patrol the past, claimed that his days of idleness were over, that he would be a man of action from now on, getting very excited, waving his arms about.

"They succeeded with you!" his father exclaimed. "Just a month and they succeeded! They shaved your head and took away your intelligence too. What are you? You talk about action! Action's nothing, pah!"

"You'd rather be dead drunk than act!"

"So I would! Though not on this Indian muck, for preference. Pity you were illiterate, or you'd remember what Wordsworth said."

"To hell with bloody Wordsworth!"

"I'll tell you what bloody Wordsworth said!"

"I don't want to know what he said!"

"I'm going to tell you just the same!" He rose and started shouting at Bush. Bush jumped up and grabbed his father's wrists. They stood glaring at each other as the old man recited:

> *"Action is transitory – a step, a blow,*
> *The motion of a muscle, this way or that –*
> *'Tis done, and in the after-vacancy.*
> *We wonder at ourselves like men betrayed:*
> *Suffering is permanent, obscure and dark,*
> *And shades the nature of infinity.*

"How about that then, eh?"

"Bloody unidirectional nonsense!" Pushing his father away, he staggered out of the room. He was going to trick them all. They didn't realize that everything that happened was part of being an artist. Wordsworth should have had enough sense to recognize his own fallacy: action was as much a part of suffering as inaction.

In the inaction of the next two days, he found another goad to suffer with. He had fallen in with the course of events, he told himself, not only because it might work to his advantage, but because by so doing he gained some security for his father. But if the government patronage only extended to whisky, it was not going to help a great deal; he had, in fact, set his father on an abrupt downward path.

It was when they were all well embarked upon the second bottle of Black Wombat that James Bush switched on the television. A view of peaceful countryside swam into the bowl; over it was superimposed a message, "Stand By for an Important Announcement"; a military band played.

"Treason!" Bush exclaimed. He went down on his knees before the set, fiddling with the controls.

A man with two heads appeared. They merged into one as Bush twiddled and he said, "Following severe disturbances up and down the country, martial law was declared last night in all big cities. The so-called government of General Bolt has proved itself ineffective. This morning, representatives of the Popular Action party took over governmental headquarters after limited military action. The welfare of our country is now in the hands of Admiral Gleason, who will exercise complete command over the government and armed forces, pending the restoration of normal governmental procedures. Admiral Gleason will speak to the nation now. Admiral Gleason!"

Amid the noise of drums, the viewpoint switched to a room in which a broad old man in uniform stood behind a desk. The cameras moved in until only his head and shoulders could be seen. He had a heavy and inflexible face, the expression of which did not alter during his brief speech. His large obtrusive jaw bit his sentences out of his mouth, while the tone of them carried a reminder for Bush of Sergeant Pond's growl.

"We live in an uncertain time of transition. We must all accept severe restrictions if we are to pull through the next critical year successfully. Popular Action, the party I represent, has stepped in to ensure that the nation emerges successfully from its troubles. The corrupt régime which we have overthrown concealed from us all how bankrupt we are. General Bolt was a traitor. We have documentary evidence that he was about to flee to India, taking with him illegally acquired bullion and art treasures. It was my painful duty to witness the execution of General Bolt yesterday evening, carried out in full legality on behalf of the people of this nation.

"I ask you all to give me your full co-operation. Action is the party of the people, but Action cannot brook any ill-advised activity from the people at this grave time. All traitors who supported Bolt will be rounded up for trial within the next few days; you are asked to assist in their arrest. I will not beat about the bush. I have to tell you that we have enemies abroad who would gladly take advantage of us in our time of weakness. The sooner we can dispose of the enemies within our gates, the sooner we shall be able to impose a strong peace, nationally and internationally.

"Let our watchword be Union Through Action. United, we shall win through all our hardships."

His final words started the snare drums again. Gleason stood glaring forward into the camera, never blinking, until he was faded out and James Bush reached over his son's shoulder and switched the bowl off.

"Sounds as if he's going to be worse than Bolt was," Mrs Annivale said gloomily.

"Bolt was one of the moderates," James said. "He'll knock out all this mind-travel, you wait and see!"

He uttered this warning in a sort of gloating tone that instantly offended Bush.

"Let's hope that Action is transitory, then, Dad, just as your old poet claimed!"

The atmosphere in the house was too claustrophobic; his studio was still a shambles from the occasion when he had wrecked it. His head heavy from the drink, he went out for an aimless walk. Whoever was boss of the ant heap, his business would still be to kill Silverstone – unless Howes and Stanhope gave him fresh orders. Unthinkingly, he found his way back to the stagnant pond. The ruined building lay quiet and sinister; had he really heard those four men plotting the killing of Bolt, or was the incident some strange sort of precognition?

Becalmed, Bush stood on the frowsty bank, watching a pair of frogs struggle out of the water in a manner reminiscent of the lungfishes away back in the Devonian. He built, in his mind, huge moving scenic SKGs with grandiose titles like "The Course of Evolution" in which flippers moved and transformed into legs which turned into wings which turned into waves which turned into flippers.

His own mysterious and possibly cyclic mental shifts in due course went through another phase. The truck returned for him; his leave was up. He said goodbye to his father and Mrs Annivale and climbed aboard. But it was all distant. They, too, might as well have been patterns in a stratum of compressed sunlight. He seemed already to be falling into the early stages of the hypnagogic state that Wenlock discipline required.

And in the strange and brutal misery he conspired in at the barracks, he was still remote.

As they drove into the familiar square and the boom lowered behind them, Bush saw that there were shadowy future figures here. This place was being watched; but he wondered if they hoped for the collapse or the survival of the new régime.

Climbing from the truck, he stood for a moment to watch a squad march by. It was one of the new units, formed only two days before, and had yet to learn the secret of moving in formation. Sergeant Pond, at his hoarsest and most foul-mouthed, was scaring the wits out of the recruits in an honest attempt to transform them into automata. Bolt, Gleason, or no matter who, Pond held his own little acre of tyranny secure.

The squad halted clumsily to his order. One recruit's cap fell off. Bush stared at the man. He recognized the scabby face. It was unlikely – with the shaven head, it was difficult to be sure –

but after all, the régime was roping in layabouts from the past…
It assuredly was Lenny, sweating it out in Pond's new squad.

Bush mentioned the matter to Howes when he came before
the captain. Howes nodded, barked an order to a corporal
standing by, and five minutes later Lenny was standing rigidly
at his version of attention before them, his dimples dug deep, his
gaze going anxiously from Howes to Bush and back again.

He had been caught in the early Jurassic by a couple of plain-
clothes patrollers, "causing a disturbance". They had brought
him back with them; the rest of his gang had escaped.

Lenny denied he knew anything about Stein. Howes called in
Stanhope, since this was a security matter. The two captains,
Bush, and Lenny and his escort, walked down the passage to a
small empty room. Lenny began to cry out and protest directly
he saw into the room. There were bloodstains round the walls
and on the floor. In one corner stood some battered golf clubs.
Howes excused himself and left. The escort posted itself outside
the door.

Stanhope's mouth had gone a frightening shape. He picked
up one of the clubs and showed Bush what to do with it. Lenny
groaned and fell to the floor. Bush took the club, moist from
Stanhope's grip. He brought it smashing down into Lenny's ribs.
It was easy – pleasant! Action!

Afterwards, he wondered at himself like a man betrayed.
Lenny told them nothing, beyond the reiterated fact that he and
Stein had quarrelled and the older man had minded away from
them; he told them nothing, but he bled a good deal.

When Bush had washed and eaten an excellent solitary meal,
he was kitted out for his mission of assassination. They issued
him with a strong one-piece and a pack. Both the suit, which
was fitted with deep pouches and pockets, and the pack,
contained a multitude of things he might need on his journey,
including a light-gun that could kill at four hundred yards (the
greatest distance at which he was likely to be able to see his
quarry in mind-travel), a gas gun, and two knives, one which

was sheathed at his belt, one which flicked out of the toe of his right boot. He was loaded with vitamin pills, pep pills, and concentrated water, and equipped with an up-to-date model air-leaker.

Trepidation seized him when he was ordered to report to the colonel commanding the barracks. With his full kit about his feet, he stood outside the colonel's office and waited for the order to enter. Fifty minutes dragged by before a sergeant marched him in.

The colonel was a mild-mannered little man, snowed under by a sheaf of orders originating from the new Action régime. Presumably he was cleared of being a Bolt man or he would not be here now.

He had nothing positive to say to Bush, and that little he put across rather badly, scuffling miserably with his papers while he talked. In closing he said, "Admiral Gleason approves of men who do well. Silverstone is a State enemy because his teachings could confuse us all – well, not us, but our weaker brothers. They could confuse the issue, let's say. If you can find Silverstone and kill him, I'll see your name goes before the Admiral. Don't think of yourself as an assassin, think of yourself as an executioner, on State business. Dismiss!"

The battered truck which had brought Bush in was waiting to drive him round to the mind-station. Soon he could escape! As he piled his kit in the back, Captain Howes marched up. He looked at Bush distastefully. Bush recalled that he had worn the same expression when he left Bush at the door of the torture-room.

"You find yourself capable of killing Silverstone?" he asked.

Bush felt the urge to be frank with the man, to be open and expansive, but there was nothing to come; he was closed even to himself.

"Yes."

"See you do then. A lot depends on you."

"Yes." The affirmative, so much more final than the negative.

He climbed into the truck. As the boom lifted, he saw that Pond was doubling his squad through the shadows of the future.

At the mind-station, he became a different person again. He was a patient now, delivered into the hands of surgeons and nurses.

They took special care with Bush. They had their orders, too. He was issued with extra supplies of CSD – he observed that it now came in crystal form. He was installed in a special cubicle (so that he could never return to his own time without being seen and called to account). A nurse with an antiseptic smile forbidding lust took the statutory amount of his blood, deftly sliced tissue from his left breast. He was under light sedation now, reciting a few fragments of the discipline, curling into the foetal position. He took the drug.

Again he was becoming a different person: neither dead nor alive, in a state where because there was no change there was no time. His mind was opening, easing back doors that had been sealed to humanity for over a million years, letting in a part of the universe. Because this was sanity, he was happy. Golf clubs floated by, a curving leg, a bottle with a tartan label; he let them drift. It was the universe he wanted, not its minutiae. He was free.

Free and yet not aimless. The drug and discipline were working in conjunction now, a sense of direction rising in him like a divine call. He was working much as a diver might work who, poised on the edge of the continental shelf, finds himself carried down into the abyss beyond, beyond reach of help; Bush was being carried back down the vast entropy slope that could deliver him – where or when he knew not, but far back into the airless Cryptozoic if he did not fight. He fought his way up the slope, swimming, kicking, directing. The medium pulled him back but he squirted on, until exhaustion overcame him and he felt sure he was about to slide away again. Then he surfaced.

BOOK TWO

chapter one

in another garden

The houses climbed up the hill on either side of the gritty road. They were small, generally with only two tiny rooms upstairs, wedged under the slate roofs; but they were solidly built of stone, and tucked snug into the hillside so as to shelter slightly from the chill east winds. Each house possessed its own small back garden, which towards the crest of the hill might pitch so steeply it could almost be weeded from an upper window.

At the crest of the hill, where the last stone house stood, the land levelled out, later to go rolling on and on under the wide sky, revealing more clearly that its true nature was untameable moorland. Walking by this last stone house, which had been partly converted into a small grocer's shop, Bush could look down at the small village, which still puzzled him. He could see almost all of it from here; to see the rest, he had merely to turn about; for where the stone houses ended, another sort of house began.

These other houses, which appeared hardly to belong to the village, were built in miserable little terraces facing each other. They were constructed of brick and stood in angular rows, defying the lie of the land, like bricks a child arranges geometrically on its sickbed. From none of these brick houses was it possible to see anything but the brownish moors and the sky, which at this time of year frequently brought rain to lash along the rotten undrained streets; the rest of the village was concealed from them by the brow of the hill; the stone grocer's shop, the roof of which peeped over the brow, could not be glimpsed even from the house at the end of the terrace, since the occupants of that privileged position had not been granted the benefit of windows in their side wall.

Bush stood in the middle of a downpour, taking in this scene. He knew that the inhabitants of this dreary place were in some kind of trouble as surely as he himself was, but as yet he had been unable to master even the beginnings of what it was. No rain touched him; he was in mind-travel; except on an emotional plane, there could be no contact between him and this unknown zone of Earth's history. And unknown it seemed to be – no shadows of the future moved here, there were no phantom buildings; the Jurassic made this place seem a desert, remote from the enterprises of the space-time world. He had been so determined to escape from the Action régime, he had minded into a fairly late period of human history – and it had been almost easy!

The rain tapered off with dusk, which seemed to draw over the land like curtains, pulling the puny obstacles on the landscape back into its clouded heart. The houses fought this process of digestion only feebly, putting out dim lights from their windows when the process of darkness was almost complete. There were exceptions to this, mainly at the bottom of the hill, and it was in this direction that Bush now moved.

Below the stone houses stood one or two more imposing buildings, also built of stone, some shops, and a church. Then came a level crossing, with an untidy antique railway station of a kind that Bush had never seen before. The main bulk of the metals curved away to a complex of bulky and drab buildings that stood away on the far side of the village; these buildings, as Bush had seen in the daylight, were crowned by a huge unmoving wheel raised on the top of a wooden tower.

In the dark, it was possible to discern two or three lights among the tangle of railway buildings; a few red lamps gleamed there; of the rail that curved away from all this, to be carried by a stone viaduct away from the valley and behind the great shoulders of land, there was no hint at this hour. Nor was there a single light to relieve the dead bulk of buildings beyond the level crossing.

Most of the life of the place was concentrated in and about a drinking house, half a dozen doors up the hill from the church, its worn front step lying about on the same height as the guttering round the roof of the church. The only sign of its function from outside was a small sign over the porch that read THE FORGE INN – ALES. It had stood and would stand there a long while, for Bush, even in mind-travel, was unable to walk through its walls, and had to go through the doors like a legitimate customer.

There was little life or light inside the Forge Inn. In the one bar, men sat on benches, their boots firm-planted on the sawdust floor. Several of them smoked cigarettes, few had anything to drink. They were all dressed similarly, in dark clothes, with thin overcoats buttoned tight even in the shelter of the pub, and cloth caps on their heads. They even looked somewhat alike, their faces finely eroded, their expressions sharp but guarded.

One of the men drinking sat at a small table alone. Although the other men greeted him as they came in or left, they did not sit with him. He was dressed in the same poor manner as they, but his face was rounder and possibly had more colour. It was on this man that Bush centred his attention, for he believed the man to bear his own name, Bush.

When the man finished his drink, he looked round as if in hopes of some sort of diversion, found none, rose and handed his empty glass to the landlord, and said a general good night. It seemed there was a murmured good night in return, although no sound could penetrate to the isolation of Bush's position.

He followed his namesake outside. The man clutched his coat collar tight round his neck, bowed his thin shoulders, and started up the hill, Bush after him. Bush observed that the floor on which he walked, following, followed closely the contour of the street, so long was it established.

At the top of the hill, the man stopped by the small grocer's shop and went round to the back of it. Invisible to him, intangible, Bush's modest tent was pitched in his back garden, among the weeds and cabbage stumps. He knocked at the back door and was admitted. Bush slipped in after him.

He had noticed when he first wandered dazedly through this village that a notice hung in the window of the grocer's — a simple house window, the conversion of which to trade had been effected by the removal of curtains and the insertion of a pile of bars of red soap and a stack of cans containing corned beef — and on inspection the faded lettering of the notice read "Amy Bush, Grocer, Etc.". Although he was unable to determine why the instinctive drives of mind-travel had directed him here, he believed that his namesake would provide a clue. Indeed, he wondered if these Bushes were possibly ancestors of his.

The back-room in which he found himself was crowded to the point of madness. Three small boys of varying ages were running and skipping about — shouting, although not a decibel leaked through the entropy wall to Bush. The smallest of these lads, who was also the palest and sharpest, in that his bones seemed to protrude painfully all over his body, was naked and wet; in resisting the attempts of an elder sister to capture him and return him to a big metal bath, he scampered wildly back and forth about the room. These gambits brought him into collision with a buxom woman in bedroom slippers who was washing a garment at a stone sink, and with an aged lady, evidently the grandmother of the family, who sat with a blanket over her knees in one corner of the room, chewing her false teeth.

The man Bush had followed up the hill waved his arms and was seen to be shouting savagely. The small sharp boy returned to his sister, who lifted him immediately into the bath, while the bigger brothers threw themselves down on some wooden packing cases that formed a sort of pew along the wall behind the inner door, and lapsed into apathy. The buxom woman at the sink turned to the man to demonstrate to him how thin and patched was the shirt she scrubbed at; this movement enabled Bush to see that she was far gone in pregnancy.

Bush was unable to estimate the age of the daughter; she could have been anywhere between fifteen and nineteen. Her figure was developing and her hair pretty, but her teeth were not good, and a lacklustre air added to her attitude and expression an unpleasant reminder of the few years that separated her from the old chewing woman in the corner. Nevertheless, she smiled at her brother as she scrubbed him, towelled him efficiently, and eventually, with marginal aid from her father, shooed the three boys upstairs to bed.

The sleeping arrangements were of the poorest. The smallest boy dossed with his parents in a double bed, beside which a palliasse accommodated the two other boys. This was in the larger of the two poky rooms under the roof. In the smaller, there was barely enough space for the single bed in which the daughter slept with her grandmother.

The man emptied the bathtub into the garden. When his daughter returned from upstairs, he sat her lovingly on his knee and worked at the table over some accounts, on which his wife eventually joined him. The daughter was content to put an arm round her father's neck and lean with her cheek against his head.

This was the Bush household. In the days and weeks that followed, Bush came to know his namesakes well. He learnt their names slowly. The expectant mother, who ran the shop, was Amy, as the sign in her window declared. When the old grandmother hobbled down the hill to the post office, Bush read from her pension book that her name was Alice Bush, Widow. When his namesake stood in the dole queue and thrust his cards through a window for stamping, the ghostly Bush peering through his shoulder discovered that his was Herbert William Bush. The girl's name was Joan. The two older boys were Derek and Tommy. Bush never discovered the youngest child's name.

He soon found that the village was called Breedale. A Darlington newspaper, blowing fitfully downhill in the wind, gave him the date: March 1930. He had mind-travelled to within one hundred and sixty-two years of the time he found it convenient to refer to as "the present". Here he would be unlikely to find Silverstone; equally, he would never be found by any Gleason agents, should they come looking for him. So there was safety here, but he wondered again what sort of direction-finding device had brought him here. It was the aspect of mind-travel that most baffled him; something equivalent to the migratory instinct in birds had delivered him to 1930, and he had yet to fathom its function.

The overriding preoccupation of his mind was neither this purpose nor his safety, but something to which it reverted continually without Bush's being able to contain it. This preoccupation was like an eddy in a stream, to which everything passing by is attracted, eventually becoming trapped there. Whatever he thought, whatever scene in Breedale he mingled with, his attention was drawn back to the brutal way in which he had beaten Lenny up with the golf clubs. That white room in the barracks was always with him. He saw the high blind window, heard the thud-crack as his iron connected with the ribcage, saw the blood souse over the floor. For his victim, nothing new – Ann had said "His old man used to beat him up." He recalled the overheated look on Stanhope's face, as well as the look of disdain on Howes' as the latter left him at the door of the torture room. He knew he was degraded; although he had never thought in theological terms, he saw himself as being in a state of sin. Breedale was self-exile.

This state remained with him over the ensuing weeks like a dirty taste in the mouth. He would have been an outcast in

Breedale because of it, even had he not been isolated behind the entropy barrier.

He made no attempt to redeem himself from his own beastliness. It was like a tangible thing. He could carry it about like a hump and be satisfied that it was a burden. What he had done had been the worst act of his life – and he preferred, in his present self-condemnatory mood, to regard it as the climax of his life rather than an aberration following his bout of military training – as something that really deserved the day of exile in the garden, when the red-hot pokers had overtopped him and his mother had proved she did not love him. That punishment fitted this crime. Typical that they should be reversed in order, as if he symbolically lived his life backwards, muddled in spirit from start to finish! In his tent in the 1930 garden, he sometimes tried to weep; but a sense that to offer any token of softness would be spurious in someone who so gladly had beaten up his victim checked the tears, leaving his eyes dry and hard as a window pane.

In front of that pane, the inhabitants of Breedale performed their own individual dramas. He thought it as well he could see only the outside of them.

For some while, in an incurious way, Bush was baffled to know what the people did by way of a living; they seemed as much divorced from reality as he was. He drew out his answer like the dole, by bits.

Only after he had mooned about the village for several days did he discover the function of the grim collection of buildings on the other side of the railway lines. It was a revelation to realize that this was a coal mine. In his own day, coal mines still operated in various corners of the world, but they bore little superficial resemblance to this crude site.

A path wound behind the mine. One day when the spring came, Bush followed young Joan along it. She had a boy with her, a youngster almost as pale as she, who held her hand when they were out of sight of the railway station. They walked past the gaunt and silent mine, in which no one went or came, and a few sparrows round the pithead quarrelled over the shortage of nesting materials.

The path led to a river; the scenery became beautiful. Trees grew here, putting out their greenest leaves; one hung over a stone bridge, a grey bridge that carried the path across the river to fairer banks beyond. Here Joan suffered her boy to kiss her. They remained for a moment in time, staring with hope and love into each other's eyes. Bush thought with longing hunger of the Permian, where the early amphibians crawled about like wounded things, so free from the love and hope and hurt that clogged human centuries.

Overcome with shyness at their daring, the boy and girl walked on. They spoke with some animation; their observer was pleased he did not hear what they said. The path led to a stone wall and meandered along beside it. Joan and the boy stopped here, leaning on the wall and smiling at each other. After five minutes, they turned back the way they had come. Bush remained where he was; he did not wish to see them kiss again, as if kisses were golden pledges. He was, after all, at an age when the certainties of youth had left him.

He looked over the stone wall at a fine house set amid park and garden, well situated in the valley. The wall had stood for so long that he had to climb it to get into the grounds. He walked through ample and well-tended vegetable gardens and arrived at the rear of the house.

So he came to the local manor, and discovered the Winslade family which, at this period of its history, was almost as subdued in its manner as the inhabitants of the village. Wandering like a phantom about their grandly appointed house, he gradually realized that they owned the mine. The knowledge affronted his common sense, since he was badly read in human history and could not understand how one man or family could possess such a natural product of the earth as coal.

The days fell away. Bedevilled by his guilt, Bush was slow to comprehend that the whole neighbourhood was crippled by a strike of long standing. The rust on the padlock of the main gate of the mine was a symbol of the general paralysis. Although life moved, making more pronounced the bulge under Amy Bush's apron and softening the winds across the moors, the affairs of men were at a complete standstill. Now Bush thought he knew why he had arrived here; it was a case of empathy.

He settled in the garden behind the grocer's, living frugally on his food concentrates, and the weeds grew high, unhindered by the shadowy substance of his tent. The grocer's shop was well situated for custom. Neighbours from the stone-built houses came here, while it attracted the custom of all the flimsier houses over the ridge above it, whose occupants preferred not to bother to walk down to the larger shop near the pub, at the foot of the hill. But there was little custom now; the customers were increasingly short of money as the strike dragged on, and the Bushes were more and more unable to extend credit; they had to pay their wholesalers. Bush understood that Herbert was a miner in better times; Amy ran the shop on her own. When he first came on Herbert, the man went cheerily into the shop, helped clean it, whiled away long strike hours talking to his wife's customers. In a few weeks, however, the customers became less talkative and clearly vexed at being allowed to have nothing on account. Herbert began to smile less, and took to staying away from the shop. He induced his daughter to go long walks over the moor with him; once Bush followed them some of the way, watching their two silhouettes on the bare skyline, the girl's tagging farther and farther behind; Joan clearly did not relish these walks. When she gave them up, Herbert gave his up as well, and took to standing about in the sloping street with the other men in creased trousers, saying little, doing nothing.

One morning, there was a meeting outside the church, and the owner of the manor came and spoke, standing with half a dozen officials on the raised walk by the church while the men crowded in the road. Bush had no way of knowing what was said, but the men did not go back to work. He was cut off from his surroundings. Yet, in his growing emotional involvement with them, he saw something to be preferred to the situation that had prevailed in his own time, when he had been in touch with events, able to influence them, and yet had felt emotionally isolated from all that went on.

Amy was growing nearer her time. She spent most of her day in the shop, which was barer now, and dusty. She seemed to have abdicated from the family; Joan was left to look after grandmother and children. Nor did she pay any attention to her husband, who in turn stayed more and more away from the house. They were strangers to each other.

Only in the evenings did Herbert return, when Joan was there. Although she worked harder now, the girl carried a little of spring in her cheeks, inspired perhaps by her boyfriend. Now that his wife was so unresponsive, Herbert seemed to need more and more attention from Joan. He helped her wash the children and undertook to get the daily breakfast of tea and bread and jam. Amy retired to bed early, before the old creaking grandmother went, and then Herbert would put his arm round his daughter's waist and draw her down to look at the ailing accounts of the shop; sometimes he gave the figures up altogether, sitting clutching the girl's hand and staring into her eyes. Once on these occasions, Joan said something in protest and pulled herself away as if she would leave the room. Herbert jumped up and caught her and kissed her as if to placate her, but when he got his arms about her, she slipped dextrously away and ran upstairs. Herbert stood where he was a long while, at one point staring about him with an expression of fear on his face so ghastly that Bush also took fright, alarmed for a moment that he might through some magical agency have become visible to the man; but it was in Herbert Bush's own mind that the object of his fright lay.

The boys grew more neglected, fishing in the stream or playing with other little hooligans in the gutter. Amy lived in her shop, often regarding her husband as if she had never seen him before. Prompted by Herbert's interest in his daughter, Bush recalled what someone had said long ago about incest: that the tabu on it which began primitive man's isolation from his fellow hominids had led to the growth of individual consciousness, from whence sprang all civilization. If endogamy had been still the rule in 1930, Amy and Herbert might have been first cousins, or perhaps even brother and sister, in which case a lifelong acquaintanceship might have made them less strangers to each other now.

One outward cause of their trouble revealed itself on a day when Bush had been down at the lower end of Breedale. He now knew everyone by sight, and was interested enough in their affairs to spend much of the day moving in and out of their dwelling places, absorbing with equal relish both that which had a period and that which had an eternal flavour. Returning to the little grocer's, he saw the weekly wholesale delivery van standing outside it; by now he had been here long enough to recognize the name of the Darlington firm on its battered side. Entering the shop by the front door, Bush found nobody inside. He walked through to the back — by now his identification with the era was so close that he no longer went through objects if he could avoid doing so — and found Amy and Herbert closeted with a stranger, a plump man in a smart suit who was rising from the table hat in hand, tucking some documents into an inside pocket. Bush did not care for the look of him, and noted that he was smiling in a strained way, whereas Amy had broken down on her side of the table and was weeping. Herbert stood helplessly beside his wife, clutching her shoulder.

A legal document lay on the table. Bush glanced at it before Amy took it up. From the little he saw of it, he gathered that she had had to sell her business to the larger firm. Presumably they had grown too much in debt for her to take any other course. He looked down at Amy, feeling the shock and sorrow of it.

The plump man found his own way out. Amy sat at the table and stifled her tears while Herbert paced about, two paces one way, two the other.

Amy recovered herself and stood up, saying something to Herbert in a brusque manner. He replied, gesturing. At once, they were in the midst of a mighty row, perhaps the grimmest they had ever had. By her gestures, which included a lot of pointing down the hill, Bush gathered she was in some way including the mine in her abuse – the mine that with its dark closed alleys underground bulked large in all their lives.

The row grew more violent. Amy snatched up a lesson book from the table and flung it at Herbert. She was too close in the tiny room to miss; it hit him in the corner of the mouth.

He leapt at her, grasped her with both hands about the throat. Bush threw himself forward, fell through them with his hands waving, and struck his head a blow on the chimney breast. As he staggered to one side, Herbert threw Amy to the floor. Then he ran out of the back door, slamming it behind him.

Bush leant against the wall on which he had struck himself. It felt at once glassy and rubbery, like any object through the entropy barrier. He clutched at his air-leaker, breathing painfully. His head rang, but already he was glad he had jumped instinctively to the woman's aid. He opened one eye and gazed down at her. She was doubled up with the pangs of birth.

Forgetting his own woes, he hurried out to the street. Nobody was about. The hour was two in the afternoon, when everyone sat in their parlours, pretending they had lunched adequately, or in the pub, forgetting they had lunched inadequately. The Bush children had disappeared; nor was there any sign of Herbert. Nor – he realized it almost as soon as the emptiness stopped him – could he attract anyone's attention if he did see them.

He located Tommy and Derek playing with a couple of fellow hooligans in an old derelict railway truck standing on the edge of the sidings. The smallest boy was nowhere about. Granny was sitting in a garrulous neighbour's kitchen. It was an hour before he found Joan. As he might have guessed had he not been in such a distressed state of mind, she was sitting in a little back room talking with two girlfriends of hers. He stood and looked. She was so meek, so unassuming – and so far from guessing that her mother lay at home in agony. She and her friends went on talking and talking, their pale lips moving all the while; sometimes they smiled or frowned, occasionally aiding the meaning of what they said with a small gesture. And what were they all saying, so long ago, so hopelessly embedded in time? He knew her life through and through, had watched her in her bath, had seen her asleep, had spied on her first kiss. She had nothing to talk about, nothing worth recording even on such a dead afternoon. What was it all about?

The question extended itself until it embraced all human history. It seemed to Bush that throughout his life he had asked it too often, while nobody else had asked it enough. His damned memory – he recalled an ancient day far in the backlog of his own days...or a young day, whichever it should be, for he could have been no more than four... The dentist had built a little sandpit for his son to play in. Son had built a great castle and driven a tunnel through it. Son had flooded tunnel and moat with warm water from his (red, with yellow (?) handle) bucket. Conveniently, son had found beetle in nearby flowerbed. Son had put beetle in toy boat with sail. With slight push, boat had ridden through great swirling cavern with beetle gallant in bows, looking every black inch a captain. Question, then and now: what was beetle really? What was son really? What really determined their roles?

And the "really"; evidence of some standard outside the consciousness? God in disguise? God like an all-consuming alien entity from another galaxy, digesting all beetles, flowers, worms, cats, sons, mothers, so that it could greedily experience life through all their beings?

Well, that was more or less the traditional answer to the question of the mystery of life in his part of the globe. Then there was the scientific answer, but after a while that too fetched up against the blank wall of god. There was the atheist answer, that it was all blind luck, or ill luck. And a hundred other answers. Perhaps they all had the problem back to front.

For a second, a dizziness that had nothing to do with his bruised head overcame Bush. It was as if he had almost laid his hand on the key to the whole matter; but he thought he remembered feeling like that before; the confusion into which he could throw himself seemed the nearest he ever got to clarity.

Empty-handed, he came away from the talking girls.

Outside, the sun shone, although it did not reach him. Summer hovered on the threshold of Breedale. He was standing among the poor houses that abutted the moor. In one or two of their gardens, brave efforts had been made to create beds in which to grow a few flowers or vegetables to fill the hollow cookpots; but the moorland had stubbornly resisted such economy. He wandered over the crest of the hill, staring down at Breedale as he had often done before, and saw Herbert Bush.

Herbert was tacking up the hill, almost home. Bush recognized at once that the man was drunk. He ran down the slope to meet him, ran beside him, but he was a ghost, nothing, and if Herbert was psychically disturbed by his presence he showed nothing. He was red in the face and blowing, muttering to himself. For most of the afternoon, he must have been down somewhere in the village, drinking with a crony. Now it looked as if he were returning to give his wife a bit more of his mind. He flung open the back door and discovered her sprawled on the tile floor.

At once Herbert shut the door behind him, so suddenly that Bush, coming close behind, jumped back and was left outside. He could only peer in through the tiny window over the kitchen sink, a helpless, exiled, peeping Tom.

Amy had moved. She had apparently heaved herself up onto a chair, and then fallen off again as her pains crippled her. Now she sprawled foreshortened, and the chair was pulled down over her face and chest, one arm entangled with its legs. At some point, she had torn her garments aside. Her dead baby lay between her legs, not fully born. Herbert flung himself on the floor beside her.

"No!" Bush gasped. He pulled back from the window, leant his throbbing head against the glassy wall. She could not be dead! You didn't die so simply. Oh, yes, you did, if you had suffered from long undernourishment, if you struck yourself on the table as you fell, if you were trapped in a whole skein of adverse economic, historic, and emotional circumstances; you died fairly easily. But her life – she couldn't have been born for this squalid end! The promise of her girlhood...her marriage...even a few weeks ago she had seemed happy, despite everything.

It made no difference.

He was startled to find Herbert's face glaring out of the window at him. It had lost its flush and was ashen – appeared even to have lost its shape. Bush realized that the man was not looking at him. He was seeing nothing, unless it was the mess of his life; with one hand he was reaching up to the little shelf above the sink on which he kept his washing and shaving tackle. He brought down his long cut-throat razor.

"Herbert, no, no!" Bush jumped in front of the window, tapped uselessly on the glass, which felt malleable to him. He waved, he shouted, and before his eyes Herbert Bush cut his throat, drawing the blade from his left ear almost to his right.

The next moment, he appeared at the back door, razor still grasped in hand. Blood cascaded over his shirt. He took three steps into the garden, knee high in cow parsley, and collapsed among the creamy heads of the weeds, his body half-covering Bush's phantasmal tent. Bush was running away in terror.

It was as if the tragedy that occurred in the Bush family was an historical necessity. The whole village chipped in their pennies for a fund for the children, the whole village paraded to the cemetery behind the church. Even the lord of the manor sent one of his mine managers to represent him; possibly Herbert held a good position at the pit. Some of the men spoke to the manager afterwards; the union was brought in; discussions were restarted. The ghastly deaths had jolted everyone from their sullen apathy. They were prepared to negotiate again. An agreement was reached.

Only four days after Amy and Herbert Bush were buried, the men were streaming down the hill in their working clothes again, they were being carried down in the primitive cage into the earth, they were hewing away at the fossil trees that had themselves been above the ground in distant days.

Bush stayed in Breedale, to see Joan take her job as assistant in the shop, working under a man employed by the wholesalers who had bought the business, a man who rode in on a bike every morning from another village down the valley, a scrubbed, efficient, smiling man in an uncomfortable collar, a promising young man. A neighbour looked after the Bush boys during the day. Grandmother fended for herself. Now that the weather was fine, she was able to sit outside her back door in a hard chair – which she evidently resented, since neighbouring grannies not cursed with grocer's shops could sit outside their front doors, thus viewing the street and its activities.

It was Bush's main concern to watch over Joan. In a year or so she would be old enough to marry the boy who still courted her – the boy who was now working down the pit for the first time. Bush could discover no indication that she ever thought of her parents. He wondered if it ever entered her head that her father killed himself in a moment of unbalance, not from sorrow but from guilt – but if it did, she and he would be the only ones to think it.

So Bush seemed to have reached a dead end, and gradually he was forced to revert to his own predicament – only to find, somewhat to his surprise, that his ego had repaired itself. He accepted that the shock of finding his mother dead, followed by the gruelling military training, had temporarily occulted his reason.

At the same time, shreds of moral discipline, surviving buried but unharmed from an earlier period of his life, prompted him to think that he must in future be more a force for positive good. He believed he had been through enough bad to recognize its opposite.

Which led him to understand that he must do what he could to upset the Action régime, for *how far was a feeling genuine if it did not find expression in an external act?*

He used this question to stiffen his good resolutions, so overcome by the beauty and universality of it, for it embodied truths, he felt, which he had come on in Breedale, that it was some while before he recognized it as kin to an old Biblical saying his art master had often jocularly applied to his pupils' still life studies of apples and pears, "By their fruits ye shall know them." All the same, he had worked round to the perception for himself, which was a promising sign.

Bush's soul had broken away from its little mud hut. It moved now in a mighty crystal palace. He felt the godlike qualities in himself.

This merciful interlude in Breedale, away from the real world, had given him the opportunity to find himself. It was his forty days in the wilderness. Much of the days when he discovered this transformation of soul he spent praying; but the prayers changed shape and tone, and came winging back to him. It was the god-quality in *himself* he needed to reveal – and to reveal to others as well as himself.

During that long day in another garden, when his mother had proved how she had turned against him, he had become aware of a flaw in the moral structure of the universe. Now he felt strong enough to take a patch to that flaw, to rise upon a course of positive action, to make over the world again!

He starved himself. He had visions Away from the world, he could see it glinting at his fingertips, ready to be fashioned. It was a complex work of art, on which he had the largest – purest! – ambitions. He would show his mother that he could be a god, quite beyond her petty scheme of rewards and punishments.

He got ready to mind-travel again He knew what he had to do. The lesser things before the greater, material before transcendental. There was one more hesitation first of all, easily dismissed: he wondered if he should remain in 1930, not in Breedale, but in some other places – notably in London, for it was common knowledge (he seemed to remember), and something of a joke, that intellectuals who mind-travelled made for Buckingham Palace, enjoying its snob appeal, its comforts, its discomforts, and its convenience as a rendezvous. But this close to the present, the palace would be deserted by all but the royal House of Windsor and their entourage.

No, his quarry might well be there...but farther back in time, at a time more easily available to all except mavericks like Bush. He thought he could divine the exact date, and prepared to mind there.

Before he left the mining community, a surprise presented itself. The new manager of the little grocer's, who had been there no more than ten days, rolled down the blind over the door at eight o'clock one evening, bolted the door, and turned to propose marriage to Joan. So Bush interpreted it by her modest looks, her smiles, her moment of fear, his way of clasping her hand formally and tenderly. Next day, the fellow cycled to work as usual and presented Joan with a ring from his neat waistcoat pocket; as he slipped it on her finger, she smiled with misty eyes and suddenly put an arm about his neck, resting a cheek against his head.

Bush wondered at her, this ordinary girl! Was she just an opportunist? Did she care for the young man? Was she hard-hearted or indifferent? Her external acts were capable of being read in conflicting ways.

"This is my story, being acted for me," he told himself. "When I have sorted out my affairs, I can return here and see what happens to her, if I so wish." They would always be here, perched on the edge of the great moor. For that matter, her father would always be running out dying into the cow parsley. Perhaps Bush would come back and change it all through his new divinity.

When he had folded up his tent, collected his chattels, and was about to give himself a jab of CSD, he went to take leave of Joan. She was in the back room, checking over invoices, with the old granny sitting behind her, chewing her teeth with the horrid geniality of a medieval *memento mori*.

Bush raised his hand in salutation to all bitter-sweet things; he was already half delirious from the effects of the drug; he wondered that he had frequently felt so much more alone in his own epoch, among people he could touch and talk with, and presumably "understand" better than he "understood" this little faded underfed virgin. But understanding was a poor thing beside wonder.

Reluctant to disappear before her unseeing eyes, he moved outside. Overhead, a cuckoo hurtled in a parabola towards the bare line of moor as if fired from a great feathered gun. Bush vanished from the scene like a ghost.

chapter two

the great victorian palace

He stood under great elms and knew this was the place – his Dark Woman was nearby, very shadowy, her form erased a thousand times by the passers-by. At the end of the line of elms stood a great crystal fountain, its waters pouring in a circular pool. Fountain, pool, and elms were enclosed in a mighty glass arcade and flanked by bizarre statuary.

Bush knew this place and time; the Victorian mania in his childhood ensured that. This was 1851, when the Great Exhibition was held to testify to the upsurge of British wealth and power. He went over and stood by one gigantic statue that caught his fancy almost as much as it did the crowd's. It was a German statue fashioned out of zinc, depicting a mighty Amazon woman riding a stallion bare-back and bare-breasted. She was about to plunge her lance into a tigress which, prompted by reasons of its own, was climbing up and over the horse's shoulder.

The Victorians, in sculpture and painting, had been masters of "What will happen next?", freezing one second of time into a question; their skill had been both lost and derided with the onset of photography and cinema and television and lasoids – all of which insisted on answering the question, rather than remaining content to pose it. Now he was faced with the same question in his own life, and must solve it with action. The Dark

Woman was watching him. From her vantage point in time, she might well know what-happened-next-to-Eddie-Bush. It was not a comforting thought; he was pleased to think that she knew no more than he whether the Amazon or the tigress won their battle.

There were other what-would-happen-nexts involved with his personal equation; hanging about beneath the great zinc figure, he decided that the first one concerned Silverstone, alias Stein. He had been trained to assassinate Silverstone; clearly, the man had something that was dangerous to the Gleason régime – which Bush in his new mood saw was something to cherish. It was his duty to get to Silverstone and warn him – if Silverstone was still alive – for although Bush had personal reasons to know that Silverstone was well able to protect himself, he would probably have several of Gleason's agents on his trail by now. Popular Action mind-travellers would be stretching throughout time, searching for Silverstone and any other potential troublemakers they could find; probably including Bush himself by now.

By such reasoning, his godlike Breedale thoughts came back to earth.

The obvious place to begin looking for Silverstone was Buckingham Palace.

He pushed invisibly through the crowds, even in this moment of preoccupation finding space to delight in their diversity, eccentricity, and flamboyance, so different from the levelled-down masses of his own day. Outside, the people were even less subdued. Carriages stood here, both private and for public hire, together with leathery men holding horses, or gentlemen riding them, singly or in groups. Bush thought that the Victorians seemed most themselves when these dark ambiguous animals were about. He wished he could ride one, and save himself time.

The splendid glass and iron front of the Crystal Palace, flags flying on all tiers, fell away behind him as he crossed Hyde Park and made his way down Rotten Row. There were smart gigs dashing abut here; he kept out of their way, although they could do him no harm.

Somewhere in this wilderness of humanity, Turner went about his business, the great Turner whose thoughts were all yellow and raw-red vortices of fire: an artist who was all Bush would be: consumer of himself and his age, and transcending both. Somewhere here, Turner in his boozy old age – this was the year of his death – interesting himself in such traitorous new techniques as photography and, if he visited the Great Exhibition, no doubt smiling at the horse-riding lady in zinc.

Bush closed his thoughts down. One day, he promised himself, he would be wholly an artist; first, a few historical necessities had to be cleared out of the way.

His senses were alert to danger now. As he approached the palace he was on the watch for anyone from his own time, knowing they would be noticeable even from some distance by their duller, dustier aspect, as if it was they rather than the scene about them which lacked a sufficient degree of reality.

Horse guards paraded before the ornate building; the animals on which they were mounted looked haughtily through Bush. He slipped past them, moving into the grounds of the palace, working his way cautiously to the rear, where a group of vans and carts were drawn up, with porters and servants busily unloading them and carrying their contents into the palace kitchens. From one van, Bush noticed, game birds were being taken – grouse, pheasant, partridge, and another bird he presumed to be ptarmigan. They came out on stretchers, huge blocks of ice melting at each end, the water from which stained the already impoverished plumes of the fowls. From another van, a pile of turkeys was being unloaded. Bush looked away; he was still in his innocent mood, and the sight of all this petty death disturbed him.

Buckingham Palace had stood for a long time. Even to mind-travellers, its walls were so substantial that they had to pass through the doors like ordinary mortals imprisoned in time. So the doors would be watched by the Action Party, if it was here.

He ran his gaze over the men in livery and in aprons. As a stretcher piled with dead pheasants was carried inside, he saw another man go with it, carrying another, a man wearing a blue apron and sporting a curly moustache. He showed slightly grey against the background. Even as Bush looked, he disappeared into the building. Bush could tell from the man's tone that this was someone from within a year or two of his own present – one of Gleason's agents, for certain...

Or one of Silverstone's? Bush had yet to find out how well organized Silverstone was. But he realized that whether he ran into Gleason's or Silverstone's men, they were not going to be friendly to Bush.

His best hope lay in hiding in the palace before the opposition was alert to his arrival.

Moving rapidly past the lackeys, Bush strode into the great building. He found himself in a maze of servants' quarters and sculleries – the little woman who lived at the heart of this great warren and ruled it and the lands far beyond it probably visited India more frequently than she visited this region – or was that right? Were airships in use at this time? He believed not, but his history was shaky on the point.

He came to servants' stairs, bare of carpet, and climbed awkwardly – stairs were never easy in mind-travel. On the first floor, he emerged on to a rather spartan landing, stepping back hurriedly into an alcove as a party of women approached. Three maids were positively marching along in their stiff morning uniforms; beside them – Bush remembered Sergeant Pond – was a formidable woman, perhaps an under-housekeeper, resplendent in a severe purple dress that swirled about her feet. The maids stopped outside the doors along the corridor; at each door one of them detached herself from the file and opened the door for her superior, whereupon the two would enter the room, presumably to inspect its cleanliness. In the dull light, it was difficult to tell if the figures were of their own times.

Bush took a chance on it. He could not wait about while the bedrooms were inspected. He walked boldly out past them. They never looked in his direction; he was less than a ghost.

There were doors at the far end of the corridor. He went though them and found himself in a wider and grander corridor. The hour was still sufficiently early for the floor to be deserted except for servants. He recalled that the grand Victorian habit was to breakfast on until ten-thirty and after.

As he walked down the corridor, he saw great rooms of state on one side, heavy curtains at the windows, sumptuous carpets underfoot, heavily carved tables and chairs, immense potted plants. He moved through corridor after corridor, losing his way. He thought that the intellectuals pitched their tents in Albert's smoking lounge, but could not remember on which floor the room was.

By now, he was growing confused and anxious. Gleason's agents would have marked him down, surely. It was up to him to be as prepared as possible for any trouble, yet his gun was still in his pack. He turned back into a side passage, where the light was poor.

A maid was coming towards him. Nervous, he moved into the nearest open doorway. The maid followed. She took his arm.

"Eddie! Don't be surprised! It's me!"

How long since he had heard any voice but his own? How long since he had felt a woman against him? How many hundreds of years?

He saw her air-leaker was camouflaged as a brooch pinned to her stiff-dress-front. He saw her hair tucked under the maid's cap, her face as smeared as ever.

"Ann! Ann! Is it really you? You left me at the Amniote Egg, ages ago!"

He clutched her, uncertain how he felt about her; that would depend on how she felt about him. There was a glassy feel about her, her voice came to him with a slight thinness through the entropy barrier, but she had minded close enough from his time for her to seem completely real.

"What are you doing here?" she asked.

"What are you doing here?"

"I've had a terrible time!" She motioned to the nearest room and they passed in. It was a little over-furnished room with an over-ornate grate in which a coal fire crackled, burning in a cold morning fashion without the glowing coals underneath which would support it when it was less freshly laid. Her back to the blue and yellow flames, a plump woman with a bunch of keys chained round her waist sat at a little escritoire, writing out a list of articles.

"What have we come here for?"

"That's the housekeeper. This is one of the rooms attached to the Stewards' Room, where visiting ladies' maids and valets are entertained. Relax, Eddie! Anyone would think you weren't pleased to see me again."

He didn't like it. She had been completely indifferent to her surroundings when last he had seen her. The slice of gratuitous information she supplied made him immediately suspicious. He began to take his pack off. He wanted to get at his gun.

"You left me at the Amniote Egg back in the Jurassic. Where did you get to?"

"Sweetie, I did not leave you. I went back in the place a dozen times after you, and kept asking that friend of yours — the neat guy — if he'd seen you, but you cleared off and left me."

"That doesn't explain why you dodged off in the first place." He felt the light-gun in a compartment of his pack and slid it into his pocket, hoping Ann did not gather what he was doing.

"I ran into my old boyfriend, Lenny, and a couple of his pals. They marched me off and I couldn't get away till they were asleep."

"It could be an explanation."

"Damn you, it is an explanation! Besides, I meant nothing to you. I was just one more girl. At least Lenny needed me."

He said flatly, "I needed you – then. Now it appears you need me here. How come you're in 1851?" He had not enjoyed the reference to Lenny, recalling him lying in the foetal position, bloody on the torture-room floor. If she knew about that how would she feel?

Her spiky manner was back. She flung her maid's cap at a nearby table; it fell through and lay on the floor.

"I don't have to answer your questions, you know. If you don't want to help, okay, but there's no point asking me things if you aren't going to believe a word I tell you. I can see by your manner you're miffed about something, aren't you?"

"I asked you what you're doing in 1851."

"You know what things are like, back in the present. The new government is getting tough, trying to round up all mind-travellers, take their CSD away, and confine them to their own epoch. All minders in the Jurassic were rounded up – the army works in civilian clothes, so you don't watch out for them till they get you. They took Lenny and his boys back to the present, but I got away – I told you I'm an expert minder – and I came here, where I thought I'd be safest. Now are you satisfied?"

The housekeeper was moving about her room. Although he was satisfied she was of her time and could not affect him in any way, Bush found that her movements made him jumpy.

He whipped the light-gun out of his pocket and pointed it at Ann.

"No, I'm not satisfied," he said. "You're hiding something. How did you know I'd been back to 2093?"

She looked scared. She peered at him with an anguished stare, her mouth distorted.

"What are you up to? You're mad, aren't you, Bush? I didn't know you'd been back to 2093. I never said you had been, did I?"

"You said I would know what things were like there."

"You don't have to go back to know how things are. You don't trust me an inch! *I* haven't been back and *I* know."

He had to admit it sounded feasible. But there was something else.

"You say they got Lenny and the other tershers. Which ones?"

"Their names, you mean? Pete, Jacky, Josie…" She rattled off their names.

"Stein?"

She licked her lips. "Eddie, please, you frighten me!"

He left the gun pointing at her. "Stein?"

"I didn't see Stein in the Jurassic. Did you?"

"Where's Stein now?"

"Eddie, I don't know!"

"Why did you come here?"

"I thought I'd be safe – I told you!"

He grabbed her arm, staring into her face, feeling her body against his. "Listen, you know I'm a bastard! Tell me, is Stein here?"

She turned anxiously to him. "Eddie, Eddie, don't be cruel to me! I know you're a cruel man, but I would never hurt you – "

He rattled her. "Is bloody Stein here, I asked you?"

"Yes, yes, he is – under his real name."

"Silverstone?"

"Yes."

He started to search her. Under her apron, she wore an old fashioned gas gun. The feel of her roused his emotions; and he could smell her – the first thing he had smelt for a long while; but he kept his mind on what he was doing. As he stared at her, the housekeeper walked through them and into an inner room.

"You came here to kill him, didn't you, Eddie? They're employing you as an agent, aren't they?"

She dropped her eyes, fearing to hear his answer. He saw how frail she was, really no stronger than Joan Bush despite her different spirit; he saw she was as much caught up in time's circumstances as Joan. Although he could never love her, he regretted the way he treated her.

"Ann – I was sent here – I was sent here to knock Silverstone off. You have to take me to him. You know where he is, don't you?"

She was agitated, biting her lips, glancing out of the window as if the dull nineteenth-century sunshine held a message for her.

"Look, Eddie, I guess you are a bastard like you say but – well, please trust me for just five minutes. Can you just wait here? I promise I'll be back. I know you don't trust me, but I promise."

"Silverstone is here, isn't he? I can tell."

"Yes, yes, he is."

"I'll give you five minutes then. Bring Silverstone back here. Don't say who it is, don't bring anyone else, don't tell anyone else I'm here. Just bring Silverstone. Got that?"

"Yes, yes, Eddie. Please trust me!"

"As I trust my mother."

She stared at him, suspecting a concealed meaning in what he said. Then she turned and left.

Whatever she was up to, it was not good. He thought he detected in her manner some restraint, as if someone had inflicted on her a purpose not her own – and Bush knew who that someone was, or believed he did. If Action's strong-arm men had corralled her when they caught up with Lenny, she had probably been sent to some sort of training course, much as he and Lenny had. Once they found out her shiftless disposition, her ability to mind far and wide, they could have trained *her* for the job of killing Silverstone, as he had been trained. For this reason, he had not revealed his intentions to her. His brain was working rapidly, he saw the web of the present stretching back over the unknowing past.

When the régime found he had disappeared into the centuries, they would not send her back alone. She would have someone with her – of course she would, for good at minding although Ann was, she needed someone to travel with, as she had previously travelled with Lenny and Bush.

By the same token, she would be coming back with someone else in five minutes. There would be several Action agents in the palace; she'd be sure to bring one of them along too, even if she also brought Silverstone. Perhaps they would wait to see if he shot Silverstone; perhaps that would be his only way of avoiding his own execution. The initial advantage was his: they would not be sure what he was going to do; he knew; he was going to do all he could to rescue Silverstone.

And he was not planning to stand here and be captured in this cluttered ante-room. He did not trust Ann, never had; even when he lay with her, it had been more in sport, in challenge, than in fondness. She was a tersher, as unstable as he was.

Thrusting the gas gun into his left pocket, grasping the light-gun in his right hand, he moved through the door.

On the opposite side of the corridor stood the housekeeper's cupboard, its door open. It was a large room. Two elderly matrons in white-starched aprons were ironing linen, heating massive irons on a range – one quick disinterested look showed him the red monograms "VR" and the crowns in the corners of the sheets. He backed into the doorway, keeping watch on the dark passage. He found he was looking forward to trouble. It was a way of staying in contact.

The waiting sapped his nervous elation. Of course, he could always mind back to 2093; but they would be waiting for him there; and if he sank unresistingly into the past, back into the Devonian, the Cambrian, his new-found sense of purpose would still be there, bearing him timeless company. How long was time, even human time! On the whole, he preferred to shoot it out in Buckingham Palace.

Someone was running down the corridor. Bush heard the quick steps and thought, "God, he's mad!" He shrank back from whoever it was into the dark alcove.

A man appeared, short fair hair flapping on his head, his face split into a contagious grin. He reached out an open hand to Bush. The gesture was so spontaneously friendly, that Bush was smiling and responding even before he realised who the man was: the friendliest of strangers!

"You!"

"I!"

It was he himself, swooping godlike out of time to bless his enterprise! This was a sort of exchange of love; he was overcome by emotion at the look and feel of this extension of himself, and could bring out no words. But the vision was there only for a moment before – as if taking fright – it slipped away into mid-mind before his eyes. The sight was gone from his retina, the feel of another hand from his hand. The alcove was deserted again, and his future self shuffling somewhere through the stacked deck of other hours.

He felt the sobs heaving up in his throat, and stinging tears at his eyes.

Almost before he had time to control himself, other noises came down the corridor.

In the utter soundlessness, he heard the padding footsteps of people walking in mind-travel. He shrank back, so that his silhouette did not show against the light from the open door beyond which the women plied their irons.

It would be satisfying to jump out on Silverstone as the man had jumped out on him in the Jurassic – no doubt mistaking Bush then, by a curious sort of precognitive error, for an assassin trained by Stanhope, Howes and company.

Two figures appeared, halting within a yard of Bush. He saw at once that they were from his own time, although both wore period disguises. One was Ann, still in her maid's uniform. The other was a gentleman in morning coat and waistcoat. Bush could not make out his face as he glanced sharply at Ann, beyond noticing smooth mutton-chop whiskers, but he saw at once that it was not Silverstone.

The two of them stepped through into the ante-chamber to the stewards' room. Bush followed, raising the light-gun.

"Put your hands up!" he said.

They swung round in surprise. He saw the man's face then. Even under the whiskers, there was no failing to recognize it. The fellow had a wig, too, covering his bald head. He had once bribed Bush with a bottle of Black Wombat Special. He had given Bush his orders for the assassination mission. He would be one of the men who most wanted to kill Bush for failing in that mission. His name was Howes.

So, thought Bush, if Ann had brought him, then Ann had betrayed him. Like all women, she couldn't be trusted, she didn't love him. He fired at her. She was no more than four feet away, and she dropped as the pencil of light cut into her.

As Bush swung the gun onto Howes, he saw the captain draw his gun. Time went out of kilter again. He watched the gun come up and aim at him, he saw the expression change on Howes' face as he squeezed the button. And all the time Bush's arm was coming up slowly, slowly, like a dead man's under water, and Ann was still rolling at his feet, her fair hair veiling her face.

He saw Howes' gun go off, and then he was stumbling across Ann, joining her in oblivion.

chapter three

under the queen's skirts

"You were quoting Wordsworth," Howes said coldly. "Get up!"

The retching had brought Bush round, jerking him from a messy and tumbled unconsciousness. He sat up, still heaving slightly. Howes had used a gas gun on him, the effects of which were unpleasant but not lethal; clutching his forehead, Bush almost wished it were vice versa.

Howes had hauled him into a bedroom, a gigantic chamber somewhat eccentrically furnished even for Victorian times, with a brass bed at one end and, at the other, a massive grate executed in mock *cinquecento* style, supporting two mourning ladies and a surprising number of lesser cherubs in cast iron. Bush stared at it in horrid surprise; it seemed to be all that was needed to complete his disorientation. He was looking at it close to, sprawling on a large polar bear rug, the fur of which was inaccessible to his touch.

"Oh, God, I killed Ann!" he said, wiping his face.

Howes stood over him and said, "I've been looking for you, Bush. What have you got to say for yourself?"

"I'll talk to you when I'm able to get up, not before."

Howes grasped him by the arm and pulled him up. As he came, Bush brought his fist round. But the effects of the gas had not yet worn off. He could put no force into the blow and Howes blocked it easily.

"Right then, Bush – you're on your feet! There's trouble here, and I want to know where you've been hiding since you left 2093. Come on, start talking!"

"I've nothing to say to you or anyone of your régime."

"I suspect you don't know which side I'm on, or which side you yourself are on."

"I'm clear enough about myself, thanks. Lick your own wounds!"

"Right, then, let's start with you. Why did you shoot Ann?"

It was a question he could not bear to brush aside.

"You know why I shot her! I shot her because she betrayed me! She brought you along here to kill me, and don't tell me otherwise."

"Why didn't you shoot *me* first, if I was the danger to you?" Seeing Bush's hesitation, Howes went on, "I'll tell you why! I read up on your dossier at the Wenlock Institute long before I sent you after Silverstone. You're all mixed up about women because you believe your mother betrayed you in some way; from then on, you've always had a compulsion to betray women before they could betray you."

Feeling an urge to justify himself, Bush said, "You don't know what's been going on, Howes. I couldn't carry out your damned orders. I've been out of your reach, meditating, watching the troubles of one family lost in history, its hopes and sufferings. There was a woman there I would have done anything to help."

Howes' reaction was unsympathetic. Bush had often tried self-confession before to disarm the opposition; it never worked; yet he was too set in his course to forswear the useless tactic.

"That's as it may be. You're a thoroughly mixed-up fellow. I'm going to tell you about why you have made a great mistake about Ann – and about my role in these proceedings."

"To hell with your preaching! Shoot me and get it over, or sacrifice me to Great Lord Gleason – or whoever your current boss is!"

Howes leant on the oak panelling and said, "I hauled you in here to talk to you, not kill you. I'm in trouble, Bush, and I'm not your enemy, though I won't deny I have no great fondness for you. Now, listen, Ann loved you. You could say she gave her life for you. I sent her back here to 1851 to find you and kill you before you killed Silverstone – we knew you would arrive in your own bad time. You thought Ann was a hard little bitch, didn't you? The pose was only to protect a soft interior. When she ran into you in the corridor, she couldn't harm you. She came to tell me and – "

Bush laughed curtly. "Sure, you'd do the job for her. Very tender-hearted! I'd call it squeamish myself."

"No doubt. But you don't understand the situation. I've had too much on my hands these last few weeks, while you've been mind-travelling at your ease, to worry about you, but as soon as Ann came and told me you were here, I knew you would have changed your mind about killing Silverstone – I know you, you see. I'm right, aren't I? You came to warn him, not shoot him, didn't you? I can read it in your face, man! I minded back here to save Silverstone. I hoped to get you as an ally – that's why Ann brought me back to talk to you. And you killed her out of hand!"

"You're lying to me – you're just damned lying! It was you and that fool Stanhope sent me to kill Silverstone in the first place. Don't try to pretend you have suddenly changed sides!"

"Not suddenly, Bush – my make-up is very different from yours. I've always been on the same side: against Bolt or Gleason and all they represent – although Gleason is proving far more a tyrant than Bolt was."

Bush rubbed the back of his neck and stared at the black lead ladies in the grate.

"You're mad if you expect me to accept all this. What are you doing it for?"

"Silverstone has knowledge that can overturn the Action party – and not just Action but any totalitarian régime. Wenlock, as you may know, is locked up in a mental institution, under close guard. He's perfectly sane. Although he once regarded Silverstone as his rival, after what he has suffered recently, he sees him as an ally. We've managed to infiltrate men into the guards round Wenlock. Wenlock, like Silverstone, is one of the key figures in the coming revolution. I am working for them."

Bush stared at him untrustingly. "Prove it."

"You are my proof! As you know, my job was to send out assassins and agents to kill or bring back possible enemies of the régime. I sabotaged that pretty efficiently by using incompetent officers on the course – as you yourself say, Stanhope was an idiot – and by picking the wrong men for the jobs. You – Silverstone's killer – were my masterpiece!"

Unexpectedly, they both laughed. Bush still did not entirely accept what the other said; he felt uneasily that there was some piece of evidence on which he should be able to seize to refute Howes: but he was reassured by something in Howes' expression.

"Supposing I accept what you say? What happens next?"

Howes relaxed and put his gun away, a little ostentatiously. He stuck out his hand. "Then we're on the same side. We have to get out of here – with Silverstone, before the Popular Action thugs pick him off."

"And Ann's body? I feel I'd like to get that back to 2093."

"That'll have to wait. It's too dangerous just now. Silverstone first."

He outlined the situation. The new government was tightening its grip on the country, closing down trade unions and universities alike, promulgating its own unjust laws, severely checking imports, instituting purges. A close contact of Howes' in the revolutionary movement had been caught. Howes saw it was time he disappeared – and in any case his presence at revolutionary centres in the past would be useful. He had minded from his own hideout, accompanied by Ann.

They had taken some while to locate Silverstone. He had left the Jurassic at the time of the round-up of suspected people, and had hidden in various ages, finally reaching 1901, the upward limit of his minding ability.

"1901 depressed him," Howes explained, half-smiling. "He was all alone – the girl he lived with in the Jurassic could not mind that far – but he decided to make Buckingham Palace his HQ. Unfortunately, he had chosen the month after the Queen died; everywhere was shrouded in black, everyone wore black. That and being unable to talk to anyone, or smell anything, was too much for Silverstone. After a while, he had to slip back here to find company, and we met him almost at once."

"Now what happens?" Bush asked.

"Who's your girlfriend?" Howes asked. He pointed towards the bed.

Bush gave a superstitious start. For a moment he believed in ghosts. A shadowy woman stood behind the bed, the ornate floral wallpaper visible through her body. Then he recognized her as his Dark Woman.

"We're not the only phantoms in this palace."

"She's following us. Who is she?"

"I just call her the Dark Woman. She's followed me on and off for years."

"No privacy, eh?" Howes started across the room towards her. Bush made to stop him, thought it wiser not to start another argument, and followed.

Howes confronted the woman. She was misty, little more than an outline painted in the air. Bush had never dared look at her like that; she had been almost like a part of his own character he dared not face – escaped from the dungeons of his sadism.

With that thought in mind, he was none too pleased when Howes said, "She looks like you."

"Let's get on with business! Where's Silverstone now?"

"She's spying on us."

"What can you do about it?"

"I suppose you're right." As Howes turned away, something made Bush ask, "Did Ann really love me?"

Howes made a wry gesture. "I interpreted it that way." He shrugged his shoulders as if he would have said more, then said briskly. "We have to get Silverstone away to safety; this place is surrounded by – and infiltrated by – Action agents. Unfortunately, safety is hard to find. And unfortunately, too, Silverstone is proving tricky."

"In what way?"

"He enjoyed his romp through time with a gang of tershers. It has made him slightly – wild. Then his knowledge – he wants to pass it on to the right people…"

"And?"

The captain gave an awkward laugh. "He doesn't consider I'm one of the right people. He doesn't trust the military. Wait – Bush, you'd be the right sort of person! You're an artist! He has some bee in his bonnet about art at present. Let's move – and take your cue from me. Well have to co-operate."

They looked at each other in some doubt.

"Go ahead," Bush said. "If I am going to have to believe your story, you are going to have to believe I shan't shoot you in the back!"

Howes smiled. "I know you won't do that." Again Bush was vexed by the idea he (Bush) knew something his mind would not release. The situation was camouflaged as something else, as the fireplace was camouflaged as a virgin's tomb, as Howes was camouflaged as a Victorian gentleman. He could not work it out; his ratiocinative processes were obscured by the load of grief and guilt he felt over Ann's death.

As they hesitated momentarily, the Dark Woman crossed before them and left the room.

"You don't know who she is, Bush. She may be a government spy."

"Or the ghost of one of the women you say I betrayed."

Howes grunted. "Let's go," he said.

As they came out on to the main corridor, Bush clutched his air-leaker and swallowed several times. He felt as if he were suffocating. Nemesis might well be after him, calling to collect the debt on Ann and Lenny – Nemesis in particularly nerve-racking form, for in this place the real occupants were ghosts and the ghosts were real people; under the false whiskers could be life or death – and he was following a man he did not trust.

On their way, Howes muttered a few words of advice. Bush nodded unable to answer. The hour was approaching when the piles of dead birds and animals delivered to the kitchens would be served and devoured; there was life in the palace, and the corridor was comparatively full of people. If Bush was shot down now, they would see and know nothing of the incident, trampling through his body regardlessly.

"Silverstone's in the West Reception Lounge, four doors down," Howes said over his shoulder.

Braided frock coats with wide lapels, basquine bodices, embroidered waistcoats, skirts with multiple flounces, surrounded them, and for every other guest there was a footman in the livery of the royal household. Bush peered anxiously round the bare sloping shoulders and the sidewhiskers for sight of an assassin.

They reached the door of the reception lounge. The guests were moving farther along the richly carpeted corridor. Outside the door of the reception lounge stood a man in livery who appeared to be in deep shade. As Bush raised his gun, Howes signalled him down.

"He's on our side." Turning to the guard, Howes asked, "All safe?"

"Silverstone's inside. No signs of interference. The opposition must be waiting out in the open."

Howes frowned. "Don't see how that would do them any good." He shrugged the matter off and began to press through the door, which stood half open. His mind filled with gloomy suspicions, Bush stared at the guard; he no longer knew – perhaps he had never known – the difference between friend and enemy. He only knew he did not wish to go into this room – but to challenge a man Howes presumably knew well would only be a delaying tactic. Scarcely hesitating, promising himself a glorious nervous breakdown when he was free of this present trouble, laughing at himself for so doing, he pushed through the door directly behind Howes – and was immediately seized and punched in the stomach.

He had a vision of an ugly face showing its teeth, of legs, of his right hand convulsively firing the light-gun, and then of the floor coming up to meet him. It looked like an ornate Turkish carpet although it had the feel of the glassy-rubbery floor of mind-travel. Struggling to get his breath back, he pulled himself into a huddled posture – remembered Lenny in just such an attitude – and so into a sitting position. Someone came at once and jammed the point of a gun in the back of his neck. He sat there tensely, wondering what he would feel when it went off.

"Who's this guy?" someone asked.

"Friend of mine," Howes said.

Cautiously, Bush looked round, swivelling his eyes and trying to keep his neck still.

The traitor at the gate was just coming in. His allies inside numbered five. Four of them had been lined up inside the door and now stood over Howes and Bush. They were all disguised as Victorian gentlemen, although their ashen cast of face marked them off as minders from 2093 suffering light shortage. They looked intelligent – but then they could hardly be morons to get as near the present as 1851. One of them leant down and ripped off Howes' false whiskers and wig. He looked naked and helpless lying on the floor with a gun pointing at him.

"This is your fault – I was too taken up with you to bother over proper precautions!" he said to Bush.

Bush raised his eyebrows, saying nothing. Ever watchful to seize on such things, he recognized that Howes had some sort of compulsion that moved him to transfer guilt on to someone else.

He had revealed something of it in their curious conversation after the accident with Ann.

Howes started to curse the man on the door for betraying trust, but a blow in the face silenced him.

The fifth member of the ambush – sixth if the man on the door was included – stood over by the curtains fringing one of the tall windows. There was an armchair beside him, and a man in the armchair gagged and bound. The dimness of the latter's face and the brightness of the light pouring in made him hard to identify, but Bush had no doubt it was Silverstone; by the noise he was making, he was having trouble in breathing through his air-leaker.

"Right-ho! It was easier than we thought," said the man standing over Howes. He appeared to be the leader. He had a broad pale brow and a heavy mouth; he wore a grey silk coat and had placed to one side, out of harm's way, a pale fawn top hat, which he now put back on his head. It formed a striking contrast with his clever, almost brutal face.

"I might have known you'd have fallen over yourself to join Action, Grazley!" Howes said contemptuously. The name Grazley sounded familiar to Bush: one of Bolt's lieutenants, he guessed, who had switched allegiances.

"We are taking you and your sidekick back to 2093, Howes," he said, ignoring the other's remarks. "You will stand trial, both of you, for treason against the government I have the honour to serve. We shall give you paralysis drops, inject CSD, and mind you back, linked, with us. Silverstone is coming home by the same method."

As he spoke, he holstered his gun and snapped his fingers at one of the other men, who immediately began to unload his pack.

"Why don't you shoot us here and spare us the farce?" Howes said. He received a kick in the spine for answer.

While the man was pulling a syringe from his pack, some liveried servants entered the room. Grazley's party was instantly on the alert, but these flunkeys were obviously of their age, and walked through the mind-travellers without flickering an eyelid. The room had been empty till now. They moved ceremoniously across to the long windows to adjust the curtains against the glare of the sun; perhaps it was a routine visit.

Everyone's attention was distracted by the intrusion. Bush calculated the time it would take to jump up and sprint out of the door. The attempt was not worth making under normal odds, but the situation was desperate enough for a try. The servants were hardly two paces into the room before he had weighed up the situation and was tensing his muscles for the bid. And then the future came in.

There were four of them, the Dark Woman and three men. They seemed to hang insubstantially in the air, like legless people standing behind layers of glass. And they carried slender rods which they now aimed.

Bush's and the Dark Woman's gaze met. She gave him a small gesture, raising her empty hand to cover her nose and mouth, and then the four of them moved to cover Grazley and his men and opened fire with their weapons.

Grazley was fast. He threw himself at his shadowy attacker – and charged right through him, dropping his fawn topper in the process.

The weapons of the future worked through the entropy barrier, giving off quick puffs of a clinging gas. Two of Grazley's men were firing back indiscriminately. The weapons turned on them, they staggered and fell. Bush caught an acrid smell that nearly lifted his head off. Picking himself up as he moved, he ran for the door.

His head swam, the gas bit at his senses. His action was useless. He was never free. What was that about the nature of infinity? Action is…suffering is… God, yes, permanent, obscure, and dark…like Ann…

He managed to hold on to some of his wits. He sprawled on the rich carpet in the corridor. The crowds had gone by now, had jostled in to the luncheon. Only two important figures coming towards him, the woman in full sail, bearing herself like a queen and placing her hand on the arm of her escort in such a way that he – He! and She! No wonder the lackeys behind them bowed so obsequiously that their wigs almost fell off! Groaning, Bush made ineffectual efforts to roll out of the way as the Queen of England and the Prince Consort sailed through him and he drowned beneath her ample phantom skirts.

The shock, the farce, the madness of it drew him properly to his senses. Wiping his eyes, he gasped fresh air through his leaker, stood up, and drew his gas gun, the only weapon left to him. He peered cautiously into the room he had escaped from. All the minders sprawled unconscious on the floor. The Victorian servants turned serenely from the curtains, which they had drawn a precise distance apart, and marched out of the door, through Bush. The gas had not harmed him. The four from the future bowed to him and took shadowy leave of the room, the Dark Woman leading.

Bush spared only a second to gape at them. He moved hurriedly about the room, disarming Grazley and his men; they did not stir. As an afterthought, he went round again, searching them, collecting their supplies of CSD so as to delay their return to 2093 – though they would be sure to appropriate the drug from others. He grabbed the senseless Howes under his armpits and dragged him into the corridor, his eyes burning with the lingering gas. Then he plunged in again and got Silverstone, unconscious in the armchair and still tied. As he lugged the man across the floor, he happened to kick his light-gun, which had fallen from his grasp when he first entered the room and his mind, although muzzy from the gas, started to spark off revelations at him, so that he almost cried aloud in surprise and relief.

He had a knife in his pack. Pulling it out, he cut the rope that bound Silverstone and tied up Howes instead, trussing his hands behind his feet and tying his ankles back towards his wrists.

"You clever bastard!" he said.

Then he started yelling down the palace corridors, "Ann! Ann!"

chapter four

a case of incoherent light

A number of arbitrary points mark the mental frontiers of our lives. Stake out, say, a crooked leg, a line from Wordsworth, a day in an abandoned garden, a loving cheek on a shoulder, a bloody golf club, a drug, the long twilight of a Devonian beach, a light-gun, and you define within these factors one human existence. It is an unusual human being who is more than the multiple of his factors

Bush broke away now. So strong was his sudden preception that Ann lived that he forgot all he had been taught and started inventing new rules.

After a berserk moment of running down the corridor shouting, he knew it was useless to try and track Ann down that way. Convinced she was alive, he realized she might have her own obscure purposes for being away from the palace. He had only a little while to act before Grazley and his men recovered consciousness. To find if Ann was still alive, he minded.

He did it by flexing muscles he never knew existed within the dark territory of his undermind. The CSD still ran in his veins from his recent emergence into 1851, otherwise he could not have achieved what he did.

Diving into the reception room, he sank himself back; space-time tilted, and then surfaced in the palace again – how much earlier? He did not know. There were other people in the lounge, genuine Victorians – not Silverstone, not Howes, not Ann.

He dived under again, kicking, in and out of mind. People. Times. 1847? '49? '50? He kept surfacing and diving powered by emotion, like a dolphin speeding through water, glaring out of the window trying to feel the medium he was plunging through, seeing sunlight in the courtyard outside replaced by snow, leaves blowing across the pavements, night, day, grey light or daylight. He fought his way upstream.

As he did so, he was concealing himself in one of the window bays. The heavy curtains helped his purpose. He needed to find the place in space-time immediately before Ann and Howes had come to him, when his earlier self was waiting in the little ante-chamber down the corridor. As his first frenzy cooled, the task of minding became harder. The dolphin stuck in the shallows. He stopped. Some damned anonymous day in 1851, unrecorded…although the Queen would be making an entry in her journal, careful and pedestrian, unobscured by any doubts of the universe of which she ruled so mighty a mote.

Impatient, he jabbed an ampoule of CSD into his artery and moved into mind-travel again.

There was Silverstone! Pacing a corner of the room. Bush remembered clearly that remarkable face, with the wry mouth and beaky nose; a phrase describing it popped into being: the self-mocking bird. Four genuine Victorian gents smoked at the other end of the chamber. Bush knew this was the moment he needed; that mysterious instinctive sense guiding him through mind-travel had worked again. He must be careful. He was only a matter of minutes, scarcely an hour, away from Silverstone in time. The man would be able to see him quite easily, hear him, speak to him, shoot him. He crouched behind the thick curtains.

Silverstone turned – whipped his head around, saw Bush, perhaps had seen him materialize from the corner of his eye. His face clouded, he pointed an accusing finger at Bush. Dumbfounded by his own stupidity, Bush flicked back into mind. He had forgotten that Silverstone spent some while in 1851 before Howes arrived, had forgotten to take thorough precautions against being seen by men of his own time.

He surfaced. The room was empty now, stacked with twilight, like a replica of itself standing in a museum. He went behind a long sofa, the upholstered wooden back of which curved like a mahogany wave, foaming roses and rose buds. Safely concealed, he urged through time again, ignoring his own fatigue.

Then he had it!

The instinct had served him well and homed him in on a moment when they were actually talking about him.

Silverstone was sitting on the floor, his back to the wall. Howes was standing by him, but had turned from him as Ann entered the room. She was in distress, calling to him even as she ran across to the far side of the room where they were. Every word carried to Bush, faint but very clear amid all the surrounding silence.

"Eddie Bush is in the palace, David! I just met him on this floor."

She stood before Howes, running her hands up and down the seams of her maid's uniform. Howes became tense and unsmiling, even stroking his false whiskers.

Silverstone said, "I told you he'd be back. He was in this very room two months ago. I saw him by this window. He could have killed me then, young ruffian!"

Ignoring him, Howes asked the girl, "Did you obey your orders?"

"I couldn't, David! Listen – there's no need to kill Bush now. He's changed his opinions. He'll *help* us now, and goodness knows we need help."

Howes made to push by her, reaching for his gun at the same time.

"You've disobeyed orders, Ann. We've got enough trouble without the uncertain factor of Bush complicating life for us. Take me to him!"

She caught his arm. "Don't do anything you'd regret later, David. He can help us. Be reasonable with him – you said yourself he was an artistic type. Besides, he has a light-gun."

"Ha! You needn't worry about that! We fixed that."

"You're so good at fixing! I'm just asking you not to hurt him. Please!"

When he looked at her, his expression softened.

"You still fancy him, don't you? All right, I'll talk to him, if I must. But don't forget how much hinges on the success of this operation. Professor Silverstone, if you'd kindly stay here, we'll be back in a couple of minutes, and then we will mind at once, before things get too hot for us."

"But my parcel," Silverstone said. "I can't leave without that. Ann, you were going to get it for me."

Ann snapped her fingers. "I was on my way to get it – I forgot when I saw Eddie. There'll be no hitches, Professor – I'll fetch your parcel at once."

Bush was not staying to hear the last part of the conversation. While their attention was focused on each other, he ran bent double, out of the door. Directly he got into the corridor, he capered, enemy agents or no. Wonderful!

He had seen the look on Ann's face when Howes had asked if she still fancied him. Until that moment, he had forgotten he possessed any talent for loving. The unguarded look on her face told him otherwise – yes, unguarded, just as little Joan Bush had been observed unguarded; it was the first time he had seen Ann with her guard down.

And he had caught Howes with *his* guard down! Howes – the fixer! A brave and cool and far-sighted man: all qualities Bush could not see in himself. Howes' strange sabotage of the régime's plans had been as complete as he could make them: and had included making sure the guns of his chosen assassins did not function properly. No doubt Bush's gas gun fired harmless carbon dioxide, just as his light-gun had fired harmless

151

unlasered light rather than the coherent beam it was supposed to do. It was all clear. He had not killed Ann.

What Howes just said confirmed what Bush had guessed. The fact that his gun was tampered with was the one bit of tangible proof he had that Howes' account of subversive activity was true.

He knew he could now cheerfully mind back to the point where he had left Silverstone and Howes lying gassed in the corridor. Time was of the essence – a pregnant thought! But he was no longer a murderer! He was reprieved! A good harmless creature who intended injury to no one. And Ann lived her elusive life still!

Caprice took him. Laughing he bounded down the corridor, back the way he knew Ann had just come.

He found his earlier self lurking in the dark alcove behind which the women still ironed. Impulsively he reached out his hand and found it grasped by himself. He smiled. How fine he was, larger than he had anticipated, deft in his movements.

"You!"

"I!"

It was a sort of exchange of love. How well he wished this man, this stranger whose every thought, every inch of body he knew – the only such person! What a crazy dark unknown incest this was, to be clutching himself in love! He could say no more, overcome with emotion, content with the charge that had been conveyed. He minded.

He was back – or he had been there all the while and the universe had been away. The effort of breaking through the time-entropy barrier told on him and sobered him down, making him aware once more of present dangers.

Silverstone and Howes were returning to consciousness, sprawled on the corridor carpet. Although they had breathed relatively less of the gas than Grazley's men, it would not be long before the enemy also revived and burst into the corridor.

Stooping, Bush slapped the professor's face – the face of the self-mocking bird – and rubbed it briskly, calling, "Stein, Stein!" He changed his mind. "Silverstone!" he said.

The professor opened his eyes. "It was proof," he muttered. "That weapon – proof positive!"

The words piled confusion into Bush's head. Could Silverstone know that his light-gun had been tampered with? He was totally at a loss to understand how the man had learnt what he had been through. He just stared down at Silverstone as the professor struggled into a sitting position and said, with a much firmer grasp on consciousness, "That weapon the four people from the other time used – it is proof that my theory is absolutely correct, and we shall have other proof, you'll see! This is the first time they have intervened through the time-entropy barrier."

Somewhat disgruntled to find that his own case was not being discussed, Bush said, "I'm going to get you out of here, Silverstone. In any case, I don't see how they could use a weapon through the entropy barrier."

"Simple, isn't it? We'd have developed it ourselves in a few years, no doubt. We've already learnt to leak air through the barrier; the whole concept of mind-travel necessitates it. *They* merely leaked an anaesthetic through. Now, get me to my feet, will you? You're Edward Bush, I know. We've met up and down the time spectrum, not always in friendly circumstances. I hope I did not hurt you too much that time by the Amniote Egg. I imagined you were one of that villain Bolt's agents."

Bush laughed. "I hadn't even noticed you on that occasion. I was too taken up with the girl you were with."

Silverstone's rather strained countenance relaxed. "Well, I was taken up with her too. Women are my weakness, happily. Now thank you for getting me out of that room. Undo Howes and we will go."

"I tied Howes up for a purpose. He did a cruel thing to me, just to ensure I was sufficiently overwhelmed to obey him without question. I'm not going to be used as anyone's tool."

"We're all someone's tool. That's what society means. You're a very emotional man, Bush, but we have no time for emotion just now. David Howes is a vitally important man, and we must have him with us."

We're all someone's tool... It was not a particularly lofty thought, in Bush's estimation, but it was a way of making sense of human affairs. One used and was used. He had used Ann. Howes had used him. He would use Howes. He would use Silverstone.

Howes and Silverstone had power; they could gain more power. Back in the present – in 2093 – they could help Bush if he would help them. He could find through them the liberty to paint, to group, again – he needed to create as a sleeping man needs to dream. If his art was going to survive, he had to give up some of the pettiness of being himself.

He stooped down and began to untie Howes, who was already opening his eyes. As he fumbled with the knots, Silverstone said, "You may know there was a coterie of intellectual exiles here in Buckingham Palace from our time. I have explained my message to them and they have gone to disseminate it."

"Message? Have you gone religious?"

"My teaching. I wish Wenlock were here, now our quarrel is made up. Even I can hardly grasp what I have discovered. It turns the world upside down, quite upside down. We must mind as soon as possible."

"I can't go without Ann."

"I know. We need Ann. She will be back in a moment with my parcel, which was left downstairs. How are you, Captain?"

Howes grunted. He sat up as Bush untied him, shook his head to clear it, looked at Bush. "You know about Ann? That she's alive?"

Bush nodded.

"Sorry Bush. Your uncertain temper was to blame. When you fired the doctored light-gun at her, she threw herself down and when I'd gassed you I made her agree she was dead. It's about time you had a shock. It might be good for your sadism!"

"You're sick!" Bush said. He turned away in disgust. Ann was hastening along the corridor, a large plastic case under her arm. Silverstone grasped the parcel; Bush grasped Ann. She smiled up at him, with a raised eyebrow and an echo of her old distrust.

"Why did you do it?" he asked.

"You dare to ask me that? Why did you shoot me? Don't answer! I know the answer – you don't trust me, you daren't trust me, because you daren't trust yourself!"

He lied to her. "The gun went off by accident."

"You're lying! I saw the intention in your eyes as you pressed the button."

"I was mad with disappointment – you know that! You know I thought you were bringing back Howes to kill me. It was only because I loved you, Ann, I went wild as I did!"

She dropped her gaze and said sulkily, "You don't trust me."

"We're all going to have to trust each other now," Howes said. "Because if we don't mind out of here quickly, Grazley and his men will be on to us again. We could shoot them out of hand where they lie – perhaps Bush would care to do it – but I prefer to mind before they recover."

"Excellent idea, Captain – though I think you are unfair to Bush. He pulled us both out of the hands of the Popular Action Party, and we owe him our thanks," Silverstone said. "Now, I have my parcel: link arms and give yourselves a shot of CSD. Hold the discipline in your minds, and let's get away from this madhouse. We're going to mind back to the Jurassic, all four of us."

"I thought we were returning to 2093," Bush said.

"You'll take orders," Howes said, rolling up his sleeve, producing an ampoule, and pressing it into his arm.

"We have a little business to attend to – someone to collect – in the Jurassic," Silverstone said, clearly trying to make up to Bush for Howes' ill manners.

Bush shrugged. "I want to talk to you, Ann," he said in a low tone as he also prepared to mind.

She said in a subdued way, "I don't want to talk. David's told me just enough of the Silverstone undermind theory to daze me completely – "

"Ann, let's go, please!" Silverstone said. "No talking. Ready, Captain Howes?"

Howes had already linked arms with Silverstone. Now he caught Bush's arm as Bush took Ann's.

"Let's go," he said.

chapter five

on the decrepit margins of time

Buckingham Palace: the savannahs of the Jurassic. There was little difference between them for a mind-traveller in one important respect: both lay eternally under the curse of silence three-dimensional but hardly accessible to any sense but sight. And no pterodactyls flew.

The four of them arrived together, and an immense tiredness settled on Bush. He looked with disfavour at Silverstone and Howes. The whole roughneck episode in Buckingham Palace disgusted him, as he recalled the good resolutions and feelings of godliness with which he had left Breedale. Any attempt he made to participate in the events of the world disgusted him; he needed silences and solitudes again, and reflected cynically, "Absolute powerlessness corrupts absolutely." The meaning of his weapon's failure to work was not lost on him.

They were standing by a low-flowing river, the dull blue-green jungle stretching behind them, while ahead lay plain and mountain. Nothing moved but the river. The sky was full of rolling cloud-cover, as Bush always recalled the Jurassic.

"We will continue with the plan we agreed on," Silverstone said. "Captain Howes, if you and Ann will proceed and collect our other friend, I will rest here with Bush."

"We'll get moving at once," Howes said. "You take a nap, Professor. You look as if you could do with one, too, Bush. We'll be back in two or three hours, if all goes well."

Ann waved, and without more fuss she and Howes departed walking with the lethargic tread of someone still under the influence of CSD.

Silverstone began at once to unroll a light bed from his pack, advising Bush to do the same.

"We are quite safe here. I chose this spot because it is a couple of miles away from human habitation. The captain and Ann will collect someone and then we make the rest of our journey."

"Professor – I'm exercising some self-restraint because I realize I am only a pawn in this game, but will you please explain to me whom we are meeting now and where we are going next?"

"You're too preoccupied with little things, my friend. But – so am I... I keep worrying because I broke my wristwatch and don't know the time – the time! *A* time! And yet I know every wristwatch is obsolete. I'm an inconsistent man."

"So am I! Genius is inconsistent. Do you remember your childhood?"

"We must get some rest. But I will answer your first questions." He began to unwrap the plastic parcel he had brought with him from Victorian times. "You were an artist of some sort, weren't you?"

"I *am* an artist. You don't cease to be an artist!"

"Well, you stop manifesting it, shall we say?"

Bush looked for irony, but forgot what he was about as the panel emerged from the parcel.

"We are going to meet the man who executed this. He will grasp my findings when I explain them, seminally if not intellectually. It is necessary for any new thing in the world to be interpreted to the public at large not only through scientists but through artists – that has been the eternal role of the artist, and this man shows he is ideal for my purpose. Look at this fine work of his."

Bush was looking. "It's a Borrow. He's great, isn't he?"

Without fuss, Borrow had established several areas of darkness in his groupage, interrelated by motes of colour which combined here and there into dominant masses so presented that they might have been atomic nuclei, cities or stars; the scale of the whole being thus thrown in doubt, other ambiguities could take on double or even treble meanings. Some parts seemed rather coarse and ill-felt, but they were inseparable from the whole, as if Borrow had here extended himself, thrown off the role of the dandy, and tried to face simultaneously all of himself and all of his world.

It was a groupage that appeared to Bush less perfect than the montages he had inspected at the Amniote Egg, but infinitely greater; he knew unhesitatingly that this was a later work to which the earlier ones stood as preliminary exercises. This was Roger Borrow as late Turner, late Kandinsky, late Braque, late Rellom, late Wotaguci. It was incredible to Bush that the unfiery Borrow could have produced such a statement; yet it had his friend's signature all over it, impersonal though it was.

And Borrow was coming back to join them with Ann and Howes...

He realized he had been staring at the work for many minutes. Parts of it were, parts of it seemed to be, in slow contrapuntal motion; his attention was drawn to the ominous grinding of human circumstance, to the measured shifting of galaxies and protons, and to the time strata that gathered like a ripening storm over his world. Now he looked up at Silverstone. He didn't even want to ask where they were going when Borrow arrived.

"As you say, let's get some sleep, Professor."

The sound of voices. Ann stooping to touch his arm. He sat up. No time seemed to have passed since he closed his eyes, yet his head was clear again. Something had been happening in there – his father had laughed or his mother smiled – but now he was able to occupy his consciousness again; straight away he remembered the masterpiece.

Pressing Ann's hand, he got up and went over to shake Borrow's hand.

"You've spoken for your time," he said.

"The Amniote Egg did it – being tethered there, at the command of all and sundry. I was made to find a means of self-expression."

"It's more than that. Ver told you it was more than that, I'm sure."

Borrow showed signs of wanting to change the subject.

"I left Ver holding the fort," he said. "Norman Silverstone has sounded the trumpet for adventure. It'll be new to me, I'm nervous as a kitten."

He looked entirely calm. As ever, he was neatly dressed, wearing an old-fashioned two-piece, his pack slung nonchalantly over one shoulder. A strange prophet of the new order, Bush thought – whatever the new order was going to be.

"We're all nervous, Roger, but at least the Jurassic's safer than the Victorian Buckingham Palace."

"Don't bet on that," Howes said, breaking in on them. "It's alive with agents back at the Amniote Egg. We were certainly recognized, and it is only a matter of time – short time – before they get organized and come and sort us out. There's a price on Silverstone's head."

"Then I must have something to eat," Bush said. "I'm starving."

"No time. Professor Silverstone, will you get us moving?"

The professor had woken as smartly as Bush, and rolled up his light bed. As he came forward, Bush noticed how anxious he looked. He saw also that the Dark Woman was back, standing some distance away, patiently looking on. Stifling an impulse to know her, he reflected that she was as inaccessible as the anima of his mind for which he sometimes took her.

Silverstone said, "Except for you, Mr Borrow, we must all
have CSD still in our veins. Would you please inject yourself?
I'm delighted you could come. Will your wife manage the
Amniote Egg without you?"

"Sure. She has a chucker-out to help her." Borrow was
pressing an ampoule into the artery in his left forearm and
wasted no time on polite chit-chat.

"You are going to be a sort of amniote egg for the times ahead
of us – you and Mr Bush, I hope, with your united artistic
talents. The human race has to launch away from what was, as
definitively as the reptiles launched away from the amphibians,
and I hope you two will form a part of the vehicle that effects the
transformation."

"Captain Howes told me where we are going."

"Good." Silverstone turned to Bush. "Then you are the only
one who is not informed of my plan. Take Ann's arm – Ann you
link with Mr Borrow, and you Mr Borrow, with the captain. I'll
take your other arm, Bush, and we'll go into the discipline
together. We are going to mind to the one place we can all reach
where we shall be safe from rude interruption – beyond the
Devonian Era, as far as we can into the Cryptozoic."

"You know about the air change in the early world?"

"Indeed. We shall sink until we can only just breathe."

"Is that really necessary?" Borrow asked. "How about a
remote stretch of the Carboniferous? Good place, plenty of
cover. The enemy can't comb it all."

"I'm fully aware of that. But they can comb some of it, and I
want no more close escapes such as we experienced in the
Victorian days. Captain Howes is a military man; he can bear
them, but I cannot. So, the Cryptozoic it is – and I fancy that if
we run into trouble, other powers will provide." He pointed a
finger towards the Dark Woman, at the same time nodding
politely to her.

They linked arms, Bush taking care to clutch Ann tightly. He
refused to say anything, not only because he saw that Howes still

nursed a grudge against him and might make trouble, but because he had the firm belief that he was stranded on a shore from which reality was receding like a tide. Even the suggestion that some sort of artistic commission might come his way had failed to move him.

All he could think of, as an automatic part of his mind rattled off the relevant sections of the Wenlock discipline, was the idiotic simile his father had once used to explain the ages of Earth to Mrs Annivale: the dial of the clock image, with the world being prestidigitated at midnight and the wee small hours being filled with the dread volcanoes of creation, with hands dragging round the dial to the tune of everlasting rainstorms and the quarters sounding in a bare room as magma seas rolled. Daylight came, the alarm shrilled, stirring some peptic chains to motion under the sleeping clouds. The long dull morning had worn on quite a pace before the first teeth in the first months bit into the first flanks, and not until time for elevenses did the sail-bearing polycosaurs of the Permian drop in for coffee. Only at a few seconds to midday did mankind show a leg – at which time, according to the imagery, darkness fell and the whole thing began all over again: except that in this particular revolution, five of those leg-showing mammals were going to be fighting their way back towards the dawn.

He surfaced, and it was almost as dark as it had been in his hallucination. The others were with him, Ann tucked against him. They stood utterly still, breathing heavily into their air-leakers.

They were standing on the generalized floor with which mind-travel had made them familiar. The ground was some ten feet below their heels, so that they appeared to be suspended in mid-air. It was a long while before any of them could bring themselves to step forward.

The world sweated and shivered below them, waking into the long fever of being, Great belts of rain were moving across the face of the planet, more like rivers that flowed vertically than ordinary rainstorms. The rain was the colour of thin varnish.

"The Cryptozoic – but we picked a showery day!" Silverstone said, grinning uneasily.

The wilderness of rock below them fermented liquid. Everywhere, its black and tremendous teeth were lashed by a frenzy of water seeking a place to run to. Die water did not foam or froth, though it was lashed by the water falling from above.

In all this horrid place, only one feature stood out. This was a wide fissure that split in two a prominence of rock, cutting across the dome of it like an axe wound in a skull. From the fissure, more water poured – erupted rather, gushing forth in fury, steaming slightly, smearing the landscape with its bilious vents.

Yellow water gargled into brown amid black basalts. In the sky, the same dun flags waved as the cloud-race passed perpetually overhead. Of the sun, no sign existed. There was only a series of lighter or darker patches where the suspended moisture fell or failed to fall.

The mind-travellers could not tell whether they hung above land or above the makings of a seabed; neither concept had meaning here. Their height above ground level spoke of how the earth in its delirium was heaved up and heaved down.

"We can't stay here!" Ann said.

It was generally agreed, without discussion. They minded.

They minded five times, each time sinking deeper into the terrible eons, always moving towards the period when Earth became an alien planet, its atmosphere a stormy mixture of methane and ammonia, death to human lungs. They were mere grains of pollen in a great sea.

Bush found that the others were chanting the Wenlock discipline aloud, as if it were a prayer. In all of them was the terror of the unknown, the unknowable: the Cryptozoic contained in its raging kingdom five-sixths of geological time. Each of their mindings covered perhaps ten million years; the five mindings put together carried them only into the early fringes of the period.

In their surfacings, the height of the land rose and fell – once they were encased entirely in rock – but always the rain dropped down from the air, lambasting itself into mist on the exposed slopes. Bush thought of Turner's "Rain, Steam and Speed"; the old man had created that after rushing through Maidenhead in a steam train! Here they dwindled into a three-dimensional Turner that protracted itself through pre-phanerozoic time.

On the fifth surfacing, the minders came upon a period of drought, when the gloomy layers of cloud no longer drained their juices onto the landscape. Whether this was the truce of a day or an age, they could not tell; indeed, they had passed that metempirical point at which the old human connotations of time, formed in the overmind, had meaning or relevance.

They could only stand numbly and stare at the inscrutable georama about them.

None of them doubted that the silence encasing them here was a true representation of the world beyond the time-entropy barrier. It was a panorama dedicated to silence; they stood hushed in it, swathed in its vastness, like five ants coped inside the ruins of a cathedral.

As their ears were baffled, so were their eyes. They stood amid a morphic enigma in which the rules of perspective were as powerless as the laws of acoustics or the whims of time.

The clayey rocks about them were each the size of a small mountain, with nothing less than a slab of Stonehenge. They lay heaped about meaninglessly – and yet with a terrible meaning that hinted of the force that had flung them here. They were grey, without strata, their edges crumbled by the energies of water. Everywhere about, they made a confusion of angles, while underneath them lay snares of shadow. They seemed, under the bare yellow net of cloud, to be something between the inorganic and the organic, to belong neither to the mineral nor the animal kingdom. It was as if they lay here on the decrepit margins of time embodying all the amazing forms the world was to carry, as if the raw turbulent earth itself were having a nightmare of stone about the progeny that would swarm on it. These copromorphic things had the suggested forms of elephants, seals, walruses, skulls, diplodoci, strange squamata and sauropods, hippos, beetles, finny turtles, snails, eggs, duck, bats, killer sharks, octopoidal fragments, trachodonts, penguins, shovel-tusked mastodons, woodlice, foetuses and faeces, living and dying; and there were reminders of the human physique too: torsos appearing, thighs, groins lightly hollowed, backbones, breasts, suggestions of hands and fingers, knees, massive shoulders, phallic shapes: all distinct and yet merged with the stranger anatomies about them in some unfathomable splanchnic agony of nature – and all moulded mindlessly out of a grey putty, without thought turned out, without thought to be disintegrated. They stretched as far as the eye could see, piled on top of each other, seeming in their multitudinousness to imply that they covered the globe.

The minders stared about them in a terror approaching joy, as if emotions too ran in a vortex, in a circle with the clock. Wisely, they could not speak. For these uncreated promises in clay there were no words.

Bush saw that the Dark Woman once more stood among them. He felt that there was an element in the air that made the eyes prickle and caught in the throat. It made no difference. They had to gulp down, to digest somehow, these cryptadia round them before they could pursue their own preoccupations.

But he was the first one to speak, to gasp out anything.

"So this is how the world began!"

"No, this is how it ended," Silverstone said. He stared at them with the look of self-deprecation on his face. "We are in the Cryptozoic all right, but it stands at the end of Earth's history, not at the beginning as you have believed."

And he started to tell them.

chapter six

the himalayan generation

I have to tell you of a revolution in thinking so great (Silverstone said) that it is hardly likely that any of us standing here will ever be capable of adjusting to it fully in our lifetimes. The generation contemporary with Einstein was unable to grasp the revolution he ushered in; with all humility, we are now faced with something much greater.

You notice I say "Revolution in thinking", and it will be helpful if you never forget that that is what it is. It is not a turning upside-down of all natural laws, although it often seems like it. The error that has deluded us until now has been in men's minds, not in the external world.

Although what I have to tell you is confusing, you will find it less so if you reflect first on the simple but neglected fact that we know only of the external world – the universe, our back gardens or our fingernails – through our senses. We know, in other words, only external-world-plus-observer, universe-plus-observer, back-garden-plus-observer, fingernails-plus-observer. This remains true even when we interpose instruments between the observed object and our senses. But what mankind had never taken into account until now is the extent to which the observer has managed to distort the external object and to found a great mountain of science and civilization on the distortion.

So much by way of preface. Now I will tell you as concisely and simply as I can what this revolution in thinking is.

Working with Anthony Wenlock – and later, I fear, working against him – I and my associates have discovered the true nature of the undermind. The undermind, as you know, is the ancient core, historically speaking, of the brain; its counterpart existed before man became sapiens and exists in the higher mammals. The overmind is a much later development, an amazing structure that was unique in its ratiocinative powers until it fathered the computer; but we have cause to believe that its reason for existence has been *to distort and conceal the real nature of time* from mankind. We now have absolute proof – indeed, absolute proof has always existed, but has never been recognized as such – that what we regard as the flow of time in fact moves in the opposite direction to its apparent one.

You know that Wenlock shook up our old views of time. He refuted the old unidirectional idea and with it the spatialization of time. I have no new time theory to replace his; all I am fundamentally qualified to speak about is the human mind. But I have to tell you that our findings on the mind indicate clearly that time is flowing in the direction you would call backwards.

Wenlock and I started with more or less the same thought on the matter – an old thought. Even the great Sigmund Freud of the nineteenth century had a glimpse of it. He says somewhere that unconscious mental processes are timeless – his "unconscious" was a sort of parody of our undermind; elsewhere he says something to the effect that "we have made far too little use in our theory of the fact that repressed feelings remain unaltered by the passage of time". It was the nearest Freud came to saying that repressions, seated in the ancient part of the brain, are immune to the sort of time invented by the overmind.

The next century – the twentieth – was completely time-obsessed, multitudes of people suffering from schizophrenia, as the division between overmind and undermind became more apparent. As so often happens, artists were first to reveal the time-obsession, or to speak of it in revealed terms: painters such as Duchamps and Degas and Picasso, and writers such as Thomas Mann, Olaf Stapledon, Proust, Wells, Joyce, and Woolf. Then the scientists followed, uncovering smaller units of time, the millisecond, the nanosecond and the attosecond, establishing them all as viable units with their own scale of events. At the beginning of our own century, we have seen inflated time come into common currency – we talk happily of megaseconds and gigaseconds, and find it convenient to think of the solar system as entering into existence some 150,000 teraseconds ago. The greatest novelist of our age, Marston Orston, created in *Fullbright* a deliberately unfinished novel of over four million words that solely concerns the actions of a young girl rising to open her bedroom window. The groupages of our time-dwelling friend Borrow will, I feel sure, prove equally momentous.

All these things are symptoms of the overmind's increasingly desperate efforts, swinging one way and another, to maintain its lying command over the undermind. My findings completely finish its dominance. I happen to come along as an instrument of its downfall; I am merely the culmination of a process that, with hindsight, we can see has been going on a long time. The fourth-century Saint Augustine has a famous passage in his *Confessions*, "In te, anime meus, tempora metior – It is in you, my mind, that I measure time. I do not measure the things themselves whose passage produced the impress; it is the impress that I measure when I measure time. Thus either that is what time is, or I am not measuring time at all." Augustine almost hit on the truth, and genius – always most closely in contact with its undermind – has often seemed to suspect the truth.

But you see I tell you all this in the old terms, in the way in which we have been accustomed all our lives. Now I'm going to paraphrase it in its true terms, according to our proper time concept, as our children will learn it.

After Wenlock and Silverstone's day, the true nature of time was lost, and it was believed to run backwards. Because the truth as yet lay only just under the surface, this was a time of great unrest, with the scientists occupying their thought with inflated time scales, while a novelist of the period, Marston Orston, filled a four-million word novel with an account of a girl getting up to open her bedroom window. Earlier novelists, too, such as Proust and Mann, and painters like Picasso, manifested the time-distortion that was being digested by society. Many members of that society, unable to agree that time flowed backwards, became mentally ill, often with schizophrenia.

Society coped with the problem by slowing down its pace and abandoning fast modes of transport such as the aeroplane and automobile. At the beginning of a more leisurely age stands the psychoanalyst Freud, who clearly grasped much of the temporal disturbance, although he never fathomed its cause. After him, the idea of the undermind becomes hazy indeed.

Over the centuries, the human population itself drops, and the disturbing truths of the undermind are almost buried, although occasional geniuses suspect them, so that the fourth century Augustine almost comes within an ace of the reality.

Well, my friends, such is the matter briefly. I've given it to you without much of a how and certainly no "why", but I know it is appalling and indigestible stuff. Before we go any further, perhaps you would like to ask me some questions.

Silverstone had risen to address his four companions, who had as instinctively settled themselves down among the cryptic grey forms, looking upwards into his face as they listened. When he fell silent, they all dropped their gaze to the ambiguous rock.

Howes was first to speak. "St Augustine – he was some kind of nut, wasn't he?" He laughed. "So we rescued you so that you could tell the world that we've had time back to front all these years."

"Correct. Both Bolt and Gleason want me out of the way."

"Well, it's certainly a theory to overthrow just about any government you care to name." And he laughed again. Bush thought that this remark of Howes, showed a certain coarse limitation of his mind. But, as interpreters of Silverstone's discovery, he and Borrow would have to overcome precisely that sort of limitation. His mind ran lightly over the new prospects; he realized with a tremor that in his own thinking the prospect of time and life flowing backward had not been without a place. He would have to put himself intellectually on the professor's side, to help him gain the credence and comprehension of the others.

"If the so-called future is actually the past, while the past becomes our future, Professor," he said, "this seems to give you a pivotal function. Instead of regarding you as the great discoverer of the true nature of the undermind, we should rather regard you as the great forgetter, shouldn't we?"

"That's so – although it might be more exact to say that with our generation the overmind clamps down with all its time-distorting properties, and I am the last to suffer from its effects."

Borrow spoke. "Yes, I see. I think I see. And our generation bears the brunt of the distortion! Here we are, the *last* generation with proper mental control, scattered – how appropriately! – throughout time!"

"Precisely. We are the Himalayan generation, the great hump over which the human race goes down to a future that we already know, the increasing simplification of human society and the human mind, until first individuality and then humanity itself are lost into the amorphous being of the early – sorry, late! – primates, tarsiers and so on."

But that was too much for them to digest. Realizing this, Silverstone turned to Ann and said, "You don't say anything, Ann. How do you feel about all this?"

"I just can't believe any of it, Prof! Someone's mad around here. What are we all doing in this God-forsaken hole, listening to this crazy... You're trying to tell me I'm sitting here getting *younger* rather than older?"

Silverstone smiled. "Thank heaven it happens we have a woman with us, ready to grasp the personal applications at once. Ann, I assure you that you *are* growing younger, as we all are, although the revolution in thought is so great that only succeeding generations will be able to appreciate it fully. I believe you will understand all the implications much more easily if we talk about the cosmic scale first, and look at the wider universe as we can now see it through the eyes of truth, before we descend to the human scale. Are you ready for a little more exposition?"

"I'd like a drink and something to eat first," Howes said.

The coarse military mind again. Eagerly, Bush said, "I second that!"

Ann jumped to her feet. "Let me have your packs, all of you, and I'll cook us a proper meal, or the best that can be managed here. It'll keep me sane while you talk!"

"And it will afford us all relief from the twin horrors of this place and my revelations," Silverstone said. He came and sat between Borrow and Bush.

"You don't reject it all, do you?" he asked.

" 'The time is out of joint!' " Bush quoted. "How *can* we reject it? It doesn't even seem to me a cursed spite that we should put it right. A lot of people may now be able to make sense of their lives."

Silverstone gripped his arm in fierce approval, nodding violently.

"The split second in time, the attosecond – it's always obsessed painters, much more than anyone else," Borrow said. "If you regard the mind's distortion of the time flow as sick, then the frozen time represented by the attosecond is the nearest a deluded mind can come to health. And that's what painters have mainly concentrated on: frozen time, the arrow on the point of entering St Sebastian's side, the man with the glass halfway to his mouth, the nude trapped forever with one foot inserted in her panties."

"The Amazon about to spear the tigress," Bush said.

"Degas' ballerinas, caught in the attitudes of the attosecond," Silverstone agreed. "And you get hints of the impending change in the painters of Freud's childhood, the anecdotal or what-happened-next school."

Bush did not want to talk about art; he needed to soak in the widest possible implications. Suddenly, he was sure of himself, almost reborn; he realized the awful uncertainties of character under which he had always laboured, half-unaware, the fears and anxieties that had ticked away inside him like death-watch beetles. They had gone; he hoped it was permanently. But whether permanently or not, they had left him clear to face this extraordinary and terrifying new thing. Hedged by a thousand imagined evils, this unimaginable evil, springing from the human mind and seeming to embrace the known universe, left him undismayed; yet looking about him, he saw he was the only one to stand ready for the new thing, because the others were all exhibiting symptoms of misoneism.

Ann, having piled all their packs beside Bush, was cooking dishes over three of their cookers and adjusting their air-leaker attachments, stirring and sipping – clearly taking refuge in small female things. Howes had his face turned from the group, marching about and scowling, maybe plotting the overthrow of Gleason – so much simpler than the overthrow of all human thinking. Borrow: already he had pulled a notebook from a pocket in his old-fashioned two-piece, and was sketching something; the trap of using art as a refuge rather than strongpoint was open before him.

Even Silverstone! Even he – *now* he was keyed to go ahead: but who could say if his strange retreat, his dwindling, to become a member of Lenny's scruffy tersher gang, had not been as much a retreat from the demon idea he had conjured up as from the assassins of 2093?

All this came up to Bush between the space of one breath and the next. He gestured towards the Dark Woman who stood some distance away, slightly above them on her own generalized mind-travel floor, and said to Silverstone, "I like what you say about our being the Himalayan generation. There stands someone from the other side of the Himalayas – from what in fact we must now call our past, or our race's past. I fancy she will be of help to us again, if we need her, just as she was at the Palace."

"The past has taken an interest in me for a long while," Silverstone agreed. "I have had a man watching over me since I was adolescent; he was one of the men who intervened to save us from those brigands in Buckingham Palace."

"We are their descendants... We can mind only into the future, not the past. I wonder how long that past is?" He was thinking aloud now. "My father was fond of the clock metaphor to express man's littleness in time. You know – the fossil record begins at nine-thirty, or whatever it is, and mankind sneaks on to the dial at five seconds to midday. Now we look at it the other way, don't we? What was reckoned to be memory becomes precognition – and in five seconds more by that clock, mankind will be extinct – devolved, if you like – "

"Evolved into simpler creatures."

"Okay. But we don't know what happens on the other side of the clock; what you say is the past. So there's no such thing as what we called memory?"

"Oh yes. Memory's not quite what we think it was, but it's there. For instance, the direction-finding we do in mind-travel: ever wonder how we manage to surface where on the globe and in time we need to be?"

"Often!"

"You are relying on memory," Silverstone said. "For all I know, it may be inherited memory. Our archetypal dreams of falling are probably distorted memories of our predecessors' mind-travels – some of which could have been so long they would make our excursion into the Cryptozoic look like a walk round a room! I fancy our true predecessors have had mind-travel for myriads of years. Your five seconds on the clock is as nothing compared to what the history of the human race may have been. You realize that, Bush?"

Bush was looking at the Dark Woman. "I am realizing it," he said. He raised his finger and pointed silently. Silverstone and Borrow looked in the direction he indicated. No longer did the Dark Woman stand there alone. The Cryptozoic was full of human shadows – shadows not from the future but the long and enigmatic past, hundreds upon hundreds of shadows of people, some more clearly defined than others, all overlapping, all silent, standing, waiting, looking.

"It's a moment – an historic moment – a moment – " Borrow stuttered.

But Bush had seen what Howes was up to. He triggered to his feet, pulled a light-gun from his pocket as he jumped up, confronted Howes with it.

"Drop that ampoule, Howes! This gun will work – I took it out of your pack a minute ago in case you tried some soldierly trick!"

Howes said, "You're wasting time here, Bush! My job's to overturn the rebel government, not all human society. Now I've heard what's cooking, I want no part of it. I'm going back to the present – 2093."

"You're staying here and listening! Drop that ampoule!"

Partly concealed behind Ann, who had now straightened from her cookers to see what was happening, Howes had pulled a CSD ampoule from his pocket and surreptitiously rolled up his sleeve. Now he stood frozen and glared into Bush's eyes.

Whatever he read there did not reassure him. Slowly, he opened his fingers and let the little snouted pellet fall. Bush crushed it into the floor.

"Let's have the rest of your supply! What Silverstone is saying is more monumental than a planet full of Gleasons. If we're going back, we're going back understanding the situation we're supposed to be tackling. Right, Professor?"

"Right, Eddie, thank you. Captain Howes, I really must ask you to be patient and hear me out."

Howes tossed a newly opened pack of ampoules across to Bush.

"I can be patient, Professor," he said. He squatted down on his haunches and glared at Bush. Bush stood where he was, relaxing only slightly. Ann broke the tension by offering them all soup.

They glanced at Bush, as if awaiting a sign to start. Accepting a spoon from Ann, he nodded at Silverstone.

"We'd be pleased to hear your new view of the cosmos, Professor," he said.

chapter seven

when the dead come to life

Not being a physical scientist, I cannot go too technically into this side of the matter (Silverstone said) which I imagine will be a relief to all four of you. Nor have I or my associates had the chance as yet to begin any research into upturned physical laws. Once we have overthrown the present totalitarian government, and scientific institutes are unshackled again, clearly all the old properties of the cosmos will be reinvestigated in the light of this staggering new knowledge.

All I want to do now is give you one or two examples of the new way we must look at things on the macrocosmic scale.

You realize that what man has pieced together concerning what he thought of as his past in fact concerns the future. So we know the earth will gradually become molten and then break apart to become gas and interstellar dust dispersing from round the ageing sun.

We can see, too, that this event will take place in a shrinking universe. The Doppler effect is one piece of evidence for the fact that the distant stars and island galaxies are hurtling towards us, and towards the time when the whole universe rolls into a primaeval – an ultimate atom. Such will be the end of the universe. So we have the answer to questions previously hidden from us – while of course we no longer know what we thought we knew, such as how the Earth began – not to mention how life began.

You will see from this that all the basic tenets of our thought, painfully acquired over the millennia, are thus stood on their ear. Every natural law is reversed or shattered. We observed wrong, and we did not know what we were doing. All our celebrated scientific accuracy and detachment was one hundred and eighty degrees out of true. The celebrated Second Law of Thermodynamics, for example – we now begin to see that heat in fact passes from cooler bodies to hotter: suns are collectors of heat, rather than disseminators. Even the nature of heat thus appears changed. Energy accumulates from less organized to more highly organized bodies: piles of rust can integrate into iron rods.

Some of our painfully acquired scientific laws will still stand. I can't see why Boyle's Law, about the volumes of a gas varying inversely as the pressure when temperature is constant, should not remain intact. What can be made of relativity I don't know. But classical mechanics are invalidated; think of Newton's first law of motion, about an object continuing in a state of rest or of uniform motion in a straight line unless acted on by a second force! Imagine what the true state of affairs is! A football is lying in a field; suddenly it starts rolling, gains speed, shoots to the boot of a footballer!

Silverstone was interrupted by Captain Howes saying, "You're mad!"

"Yes, I believed I was mad at first. Wenlock believed I was mad when I first tried to tell him something of my thought – that was when we quarrelled. Now I believe I am not mad. The madness is in the human generations of history."

Howes clapped a hand in disbelief over his bald head. He said, "You're asking me to believe that from now on a beam of lasered light could shoot out of some wretch's body and into my light-gun when I press the button? You are mad! How could you ever kill anyone in such a universe?"

"I don't see that either, I must admit," Borrow said.

"It's extremely difficult to see, agreed," Silverstone said. "We live in a generation that is to be consumed with paradox, because we happen to be at revelation point. But, you see, you are wrong, Captain, when you say that the light will shoot out of a body into your gun *from now on*. I must impress on you that nothing has changed in the external world at all; it obeys the same external natural laws it always has done and always will do. It is only our perception that has suddenly changed, is suddenly clear. What has always happened is that light has flashed from bodies into your gun; then you have pressed the button and had the intention to do so."

"It's mad! It's utter madness! Bush – you can hear him! You know he's raving and things just don't happen like that!"

Bush said, "No, I begin to see it as the professor explains it. The action happens as he says; it sounds like madness only because the perceptions of the overmind are so twisted that Newton got – will eventually get, that is – his law reversed. Entropy works in the opposite direction to what we expected. It also sounds crazy because we had cause and effect twisted up, for the same reason. The lawyers in the law courts had their *post* and *propter hocs* the wrong way round."

Howes made a wide angry gesture of hopelessness. "Okay – then if it happens the way you and Silverstone say, *why don't we see it that way?*"

Sighing, the professor said, "We have explained that. Our perceptions have been strained through a distorting lens of mind, so that we saw things backward, just as the lens of the eye actually sees everything upside down." He turned to Borrow, who was gnawing some beef twigs Ann had passed round. "Are *you* grasping all this, my friend?"

"I find this shooting business easier to grasp than the idea of the universe closing in on us. Suppose you divide the shooting up into a series of scenes like a comic strip, and number them. The first half shows a dead body, horizontal; the second, body half off ground; third, body almost upright, ray coming from it; fourth, ray going back into gun; fifth, gun button being pressed; sixth, resolution forming in gun-owner's mind. Those six scenes all exist in space-time – and with our experience of mind-travel, we know they always exist, can be revisited over and over like any other event in history. Okay; they lie there like six pictures of a strip on a page. They can be read from one to six or from six to one, although only one way is the right way. Just happens we always read them the wrong way. Am I right, Professor?"

"Yes, yes, a good analogy. We experienced them the wrong way, since our very memories were distorted. Do you see it more clearly now, Captain?"

Howes scratched the back of his neck and shrugged. "Give me another cup of coffee, will you, Ann?"

They had reached some sort of a pause. Silverstone and Bush looked rather hopelessly at each other. Perhaps because of tiredness, Bush's first spurt of intellectual excitement had worn thin. He had hardly touched his food. He stared grimly at the massed ranks of shadowy people about them, many of them, in the illusions of mind-travel, seeming to stand half in the ambiguously shaped rocks.

"Ann – I'd like another cup of coffee!" Howes repeated sharply.

She was sitting with her knees drawn up, her rations lying beside her, staring into the grey rock ahead of her, a totally blank expression on her face. In alarm, Bush leant over and shook her shoulder gently.

"Are you all right, Ann?"

By dragging degrees, her head came round and she stared at him.

"Are you going to point your gun at me again, Eddie, and demonstrate the new system? I think you're all in a dream – this awful place has hypnotized you. Can't you realize that what you are saying is just tearing human life up by the roots and – and laughing at it? Well, I don't want to hear a word more! I've heard enough, and I want to go back – back to the Jurassic or *anywhere*, rather than hear you men talk this frightening stuff in this frightening dump! It's like a terrible dream! I'm going back – or forward – or wherever the hell you think that is!"

"No!" Silverstone jumped up. He could see she was on the verge of hysterics. Anxiously, he took her hands.

"Ann, I can't let you leave! I need – we all need a woman's common sense on this. Don't you see? We're – sort of disciples, a band of disciples. We must go back to 2093 when we've got things clear and *explain* to other people – "

"Well, you won't catch me explaining, Norman! I'm not your kind and you know it – I'm just an ordinary person."

"We are all ordinary persons, and all ordinary persons are going to have to face the truth."

"Why? I've passed the thirty-two years happy enough with a lie!"

"Happy, Ann? Really happy? Not frightened at heart, aware, as several generations ahead of the twentieth century have been, that some immense and awful revelation was about to burst? People have to know the truth!"

"Leave her to me, Professor," Bush said. He put his arm round her.

"Please stay and listen, Ann! We do need you here. You'll be okay. I know how tough you are. You can take all this."

She almost managed to smile at him. "I'm tough, am I? You men are all the same, whichever way round things are! You so love something new, theories, all that stuff! Look, all this you were saying about bolts going back into guns, all explained in six scenes – "

"Roger made that pretty clear."

"God, clear!" She laughed scornfully. "Do you realize what you were talking about? You were talking about the dead coming to life again – lying bleeding on the ground, perhaps and the blood sucking back into the veins, and then the chap getting up and walking away as if nothing had happened!"

"Christ!" Bush and Borrow said together.

The girl jumped up. "Okay, then – take Christ! You're talking about him hanging on the cross, getting the spear through his side, coming to life, having the Romans pulling – hammering – the nails from his hands, getting him down, letting him go back to his disciples... Aren't you?"

Silverstone clapped his hands.

"She's got it! She's got it first! I was going to postpone the new concept of animal and human existence until later but – "

"To hell with that!" she said. She stood there with her back to the grey rocks, defying them all. "To hell with new concepts! You were talking about dead men coming alive and you didn't even realize it, you were so wrapped up in theories! I tell you, you're *mad!*"

"In that sense, perhaps we are," Silverstone admitted, pulling his self-mocking-bird face. "Ann, I apologize. We have tried to remain detached. It's a man's way of going about things. The shooting was just an example Captain Howes gave us. Let's deal with human life now and I promise you it will not be too terrible when you understand fully."

"The dead walk!" She folded her arms and stared at him as if she had never seen a man before. "Okay, Professor Norman Silverstone, go ahead and scare me!"

"As Ann realizes – as I realize – with the collapse of the overmind, the naked and true undermind's view of life is somewhat startling, even horrifying, at first sight," Silverstone said.

"The sun rises in the west and sets in the east. It acts like the governor of all organic and mortal life that, with their circadian rhythms, come under its sway. Shortly after the beginning of the year, the dead leaves stir, turn gold, rise from the ground in shoals, and coat the beech trees; the beeches then turn them green and by the eighth month suck them back into themselves in the form of buds; all this time, the trees have been pouring out nourishment into the soil; now they stand bare throughout March, February, January and December, until their next ingestion of leaves gives them strength to grow smaller again. As with the beech, so of course with the other trees. Acorns from giant oak trees grow.

"And as with the trees, so with animals and humankind. Some of the major religions of the world – which after all obtain their power from the undermind – must have guessed the true way of things; their claim that we shall all rise again from the grave is nothing less than the literal truth. At the same time, the medieval notion of spontaneous generation is also fulfilled. In the mouldering bones of the grave, organization stirs; worms put flesh on to bones; something more and more like a human is built; the coffin is filled, needing only the mourners to come and haul it from the ground, take it home, absorb the moisture from their handkerchiefs, and clutch each other just before the first breath enters the body. Or, if the body was cremated, then flames will reconstitute the ashes into flesh.

"Human life bursts in upon the world in countless ways! Bodies rise again from the seabed during storms and are washed back on to ships that also emerge from the waves. Before road accidents, you will see ambulances rush backwards with broken limbs that are strewn over the road to join themselves into a living being, jerking into a car that deconcertinas away from another car. Wreckage that has possibly rusted for years on a remote mountainside will grow gleaming, lurch abruptly into form and roar flaming backwards into the sky, its passengers suddenly snapping into frenzied life; they will suffer apprehensions, but all will be well, for the fire will die out and the plane take itself back to a civilized airfield.

"In these and many other ways, population increases. But the special ceremony whereby human life is increased is war. From wrecked buildings, from bomb craters, from splintered forests, from gutted tanks and sunken subs and muddy battlefields, the dead rise up and live and their wounds heal, and they grow younger. War is the great harvester of birth over the planet.

"So much for birth. What of death? We know the future, that the human race is dwindling towards its union with animal kind, that the end of the earth is so near, geologically speaking, that everything is tending towards the less and the mindless. So marvellously is everything planned that humanity follows that same pattern, in the general and in the individual. Every human being – and of course this applies to the animals as well – grows younger and smaller, with most of his faculties reaching maturity just before he loses the abilities of puberty. He then grows through boyhood, probably attending school to forget the knowledge he will no longer need. The decline into helplessness is comparatively swift and merciful; it is possible that at the age called twelve – twelve years to the womb, that is – the human is probably as mentally alert as he will ever be: and he needs all his alertness, for there is the complicated business of unlearning the language to go through. For most, this is a happy period to which they gladly surrender at the end of their life. They can lie back in their mothers' arms and babble without care. They hardly know it when the time comes for them to return to the womb, that grave of the human race.

"Perhaps I should add here – you'll forgive me, Ann – that the mother often experiences first pain and then discomfort over this process; it is a month or two before the child's struggles die away completely and he merges fully with the life of her body. But things do improve for her, and when the child has dwindled to a speck, her husband or lover penetrates her and siphons off the residual matter. The process is complete and they often fall in love before parting forever.

"Any questions?"

Bush, Howes, and Borrow all looked at Ann. She was still standing against one of the monstrous grey Cryptozoic boulders, staring at Silverstone. They had taken the retrograde progression of the universe with some aplomb; the backward flow of human life had knocked them cold.

"You dress it up to sound almost pretty," she said. "You steered away from the nasty side, didn't you? What about being sick and eating – and all that?"

"You can think through the process for yourself," Silverstone said steadily. "Eating and elimination are merely the reverse of what the overmind has assured us was the case. It may seem revolting, but that is because it is new – "

"Yes, but – you're saying the food comes out of our mouths on to our plates, and is eventually decooked and sent back to the butcher and the slaughterer to be made into animals – aren't you?"

"I am. And I'm also saying that when you have lived with the idea for a year or two, as I have, you will find it no more objectionable than the idea of chopping up animals and cooking and eating them."

Gesturing impatiently, as if she found his argument mere sophistry, she turned to Bush, who was standing next to her. He noted how their every movement was followed by the shadowy throng round about them, and hated the audience heartily.

"You can take all this, Eddie, can't you?"

"Yes. Yes, I can take it – perhaps because I'm partly anaesthetized by the beauty of the strange effects: waterfalls shooting uphill, milkers squirting milk into a cow's udders, a cup of cold coffee heating itself to boiling. It's like being a child again, when a cup of milk working its way from boiling to cold, and the skin forming, held the same fascination. Which way is a waterfall more magical, or more subject to natural law – with its waters flowing up or down? What I don't understand – you can tell us, Professor – is when we can sheer off our overminds and see things for ourselves with time flowing in the opposite direction – *see* instead of talking."

Silverstone shook his head. "I don't think that moment will come. Not for us, the Himalayan generation. I hoped it would come to me but it hasn't. Our brains are too loaded with what we must call the inhibitions of the future. But the next generation, your sons, will be free of the overmind, if we put over the message to everyone clearly and soon enough."

For a long while, Howes had been standing moodily apart from them, almost as if he were not listening. Now he turned and said, "You explain well, Silverstone, but you have not given us one concrete shred of proof for all this."

"On the contrary, I have quoted proof from the arts and sciences. When we have overturned our enemies, and astronomers can resume their studies, they will soon give you proof that the doppler effect is in fact evidence for a shrinking universe. Proofs will soon surround you. Proof *does* surround you, but you will not take these dreary rocks for evidence that the end of the world is at hand."

Howes shook his head. "I don't want to believe! Supposing I manage to confront Gleason and kill him? He then lives again?"

"Think it out, man! We hope you have reached Gleason and killed him! Now, in 2093, he has his moment of power — but we know he will be out of power, the economic disorders will vanish, and soon nobody will have heard of him — he will be an insignificant major soldiering in Mongolia. And if you mind back to, say, the year 2000, not one whisper of his name would remain."

"If I have killed him, why don't I remember doing so?"

"Think it out for yourself, Captain! Until now, you believed you had a good memory but next to no precognitive faculty. Now you see the reverse is true, and there seems a logical reason for it. Beyond the Himalayan divide we have spoken of, human life will be organized towards forgetting; a bad memory will be a positive asset, while I think you will agree an ability to see clearly into the future would be useful at any time."

Howes looked at the others and said, as if trying to win their support, "See how the professor fancies himself as the prophet, bringing great things to his people!"

"Wrong! Utterly wrong, Captain!" Silverstone said. "I see only that we are the end of a great era when people saw the truth. For some reason, we and those that come after us all the way to the Stone Age will be utterly deluded. I – I am merely the last man ever to remember the truth, for me there is the special terror of knowing that I shall be outcast and persecuted until I forget what everyone else has forgotten, that I shall be reduced to agreeing to Wenlock's false theory of mind, and spend my young manhood partly believing poor old Freud and his camp-followers!"

For a moment, he did indeed look a tragic figure, suddenly overcome with the magnitude of what he was saying, so that he could say no more. It was clear now where the look of the self-mocking-bird came from.

Ann and Bush tried to cheer him up. Howes took the chance to speak to Borrow.

"It's getting dark. We ought to be away from this damned horror spot – if I have much more of these riddles and these phantom people looking on, I really shall be a nut case! What do you make of all this, Borrow? You started by riding with it, I know, but you have been a bit silent lately – I thought possibly you had had second thoughts."

"Not exactly that. I think I accept what Norman says, though it's going to take living with for full acceptance, obviously. My thought is 'Why?' *Why* did this overmind come down over the true brain like a pair of dark glasses and obscure everything? Why?"

"Ha! Silverstone hasn't managed to explain that! Silverstone!"

They turned to Norman Silverstone. Behind him, the great circle of shades they were learning to think of as minders from the past was unbroken, overlapping like the countless images in a crazy photograph. But in front of them – Bush caught a movement that did not belong among the ghosts. A figure was emerging from the corner of one of the elephantine rocks.

He recognized it. Wildly incongruous in the Cryptozoic, if incongruity existed any more, the man stepping from the rock still wore the grey silk coat and fawn topper he had sported as disguise in Buckingham Palace. Bush identified him at once. It was Grazley, the skilled assassin.

Grazley was at his trade now. His heavy mouth was set, he had a gun raised.

Bush still had ready the gun he had taken from Howes' pack, in case any sort of trouble occurred. He swung it up reflexively.

"Down!" he yelled.

He fired. Even as he did so, he knew he was too late. The air beyond his left cheek was briefly livid as the lasered beam pulsed from Grazley's gun.

He had missed Grazley. He fired again. The killer was fading, minding, clearly still under the influence of CSD. Bush's pulse of light burnt into his left shoulder. Grazley spun slowly and fell, not changing his rigid attitude; but, before he could hit the floor, he had vanished, presumably to drift unconscious like a derelict ship throughout the eons of mind-travel, sliding down the entropy slope through the unplumed geochrons of the Cryptozoic towards the dissolution of the earth.

Dismissing Grazley from his mind, Bush turned, to see Silverstone dying in Ann's care. His jacket still smouldered, and a charred patch spread across his chest. There was no hope for him.

Howes was raving like a madman. "I'll be shot for this! You idiots! Bush, this is your fault, you stole my gun – how could I guard Silverstone properly? Now what'll we do? To think Grazley got back here! In one way, it was the logical place to look – Silverstone ought to have seen that! He signed his own death warrant!"

"You let Grazley live in the Palace – you alone are to blame, Howes!" Bush said.

He stood looking down at Silverstone and reflected on what a wonderful man he had been, wonderful and unknown. The professor's eyes were staring now, and he had ceased to breathe, although Ann still helplessly held his shoulders. Borrow tugged at Bush's sleeve.

"Eddie, we've got another visitor!"

"Huh?" He looked up heavily, unwilling to face anything more.

The Dark Woman had stepped from the vast shadowy crowd. Now she was close to them, standing next to Borrow. She raised her hand with an imperious gesture, and quickly took on substance, until she was as real and solid as they. The look that she cast on Bush was both loving and searching, so that he shied from its intimacy.

"You can materialize into our continuum?" he said. "Then why didn't you stop Grazley? There must be thousands of you here – why the hell didn't you intervene if you could?"

She spoke, gesturing down at the still body of Silverstone. "We assembled here to attend the birth of a great man."

chapter eight

walkers of the cryptozoic

She was a fine woman, seen close to. Bush estimated her to be no more than twenty-five, with blemishless brown skin, clear grey-blue eyes, and midnight-black hair. Her figure and carriage were good, while her sumptuous long legs were well displayed by her short tunic-skirt. But it was her commanding presence that particularly impressed, even subdued, them.

As Bush stared at her, she grasped his hand and smiled at him. "We have known each other for a long while, Eddie Bush! My name is Wygelia Say. At this moment only, just before the birth of Norman Silverstone, we have Central Authority's permission to speak with you and your friends." Although she spoke in English, it was not entirely easy to understand what she said, so curious was her intonation.

Disarmed though he was, Bush could not help asking, "Why did you let Silverstone die like that if you could intervene? You must have known the killer was coming?"

"We think differently from you, my friend. There is human intervention, but there is also fate."

"But he was necessary!"

"You four have his ideas now. Shall I tell you what has happened in what you think of as your future? You have returned to 2093, as you call it – we use a different system of dating – and have announced the birth of Silverstone. Everyone is upset. Wenlock escapes with your aid. You seize a broad-casting station and start to tell people the truth. Revolutions begin – "

She was interrupted by Howes, who came pushing angrily forward.

"You can't talk your way out of this, young lady! If you allowed Silverstone – "

He stopped in mid-sentence. A look of puzzlement filtered slowly onto his face. Wygelia had lifted a hand in a sign towards him and uttered a few words that echoed in Bush's brain.

"What did you say?"

"It's just a special phrase – a spell, it might be called a few centuries after your day. A degenerate version of it will be incorporated in the Wenlock discipline a few years from now. It will fill the motor areas of David Howes' brain for a few minutes, although the time will seem only a split second to him."

She turned calmly and gracefully, smiling at Borrow and Ann and introducing herself to them. Meanwhile, a change was taking place in the scene about them. The shades of dusk were creeping in; and, at the same time, the multitude of minders from the past were gathering to watch the birth of Silverstone – though to Bush, still saddled with his overmind, it seemed as if they were now departing, leaving the huge landscape occupied only with its own bemusing structures.

Bush moved some way apart from the others, wishing to think things out for himself. As he stood there, the great crowd dispersed. The view became empty, seeming vacant alike of scale and meaning.

At length, Ann called to him and he went back to the group. Ann and Borrow looked decidedly more cheerful; Wygelia was good for morale and had clearly said something encouraging to them. Even Howes, now recovering from his trance, looked happier than he had done for a long while.

"Wygelia's a darling," Ann said, taking Bush's arm. "She told me that for us to understand her, she has been trained for years to speak backwards! Now I really do believe that all Norman Silverstone told us was gospel truth!"

Four men from the past had materialized beside Wygelia, each dressed in a similar uniform. They carried a bier on which the body of Silverstone had been reverently laid, and now stood with it between them, awaiting a signal from Wygelia.

"You have made one more journey after you returned to 2093," she told Bush. "No, I have that mixed – excuse me, it is still difficult to put things as you see them. You still have one more journey to make before you return to 2093. Yes! Because our birth and death signify somewhat differently to you, the ceremonies concerning them vary on either side of what our friend Silverstone rightly called the Himalayan generation. We want you to come with us and witness, as his first companions, the birth of his body – what you will think of as his funeral, although with us it is a glad occasion." She sensed a protest in them and quickly added, "And at the same time, I will clear up any question you may ask. Some I can answer that Silverstone will not be able to."

"We'd be glad to come," Bush said.

"Are you taking us into your world – the past?" Borrow asked.

She shook her head. "That is not possible; nor, if it were possible, would it be permissible. In any case, we have a more suitable birthplace for Silverstone."

They prepared to inject themselves with CSD but Wygelia waved the notion away. The Wenlock discipline needed such material aids; in her day they had more effective disciplines – of which Wenlock's was really a degenerate memory.

She spoke to them, making a curious sign over them, and they were conspiring, riding, mind-travelling, stretching their minds at her behest, moving rapidly towards what they had once known as the beginning of the world.

More. They were in limbo, but thought could pass between them. Or, it was more accurate to say, they were in a limbo where they took on shapes of thought. What they thought, they momentarily were. Since they were in each other's mental flow, they had no existence except as thought-shapes.

"All mind communicates," came Wygelia's thought, spraying out to them like a great shrub in blossom. "It is by drawing on a fraction of that vast power that we can mind-travel at all. Did you never wonder where the forces behind mind-travel lurked? Once, there was a time when the race of man always communicated mind to mind, as we do at present; but now – I mean in my day, which is separated by only a few years from yours – humanity is past the full glory and sinking into the sunset: or the Himalayas, to use that telling phrase."

But the pallid metaphors of speech here became the thing itself, so that for a timeless moment they were embodied in the untiring myriad generations of men and women who trooped down into the dull cindery glow beyond the clouds over the highest mountains.

Ann's thoughts came small and lonely, but alive, like dancing shoes on an empty dance floor. "Wygelia, you are part of the splendid reality Norman Silverstone only glimpsed!" Behind the dancing shoes trailed streamers, speaking of her admiration for the younger woman and her abilities; and behind the streamers, a silver boomerang, singing, "And I don't even feel jealous of your special relationship with Eddie."

Back came Wygelia's thoughts, complex as a snowflake but spinning with her humour and coloured with her laughter and mischief: "You shouldn't feel jealous – I am what you would call the granddaughter of your union with Eddie!"

And they were all full of a concerto of shapes that expressed the mixed emotions, delight and some embarrassment and surprise – and here some little obsidian cubes of protest – originating from Ann and Bush, coalescing with a sort of nuptial sprightliness.

This whole amazing experience was rendered more amazing because Borrow was filling enormous multi-dimensional spaces with abstract thought, turning himself into replicated bars of mental energy that formed an enormous and transient art work; and at the same time, Howes was conducting a separate thought-exchange with Wygelia. His question, flowing like gravel, demanded to know where they were going; her answer, vivid and electric, meant: "You know we are already many thousands of millions of years beyond Phanerozoic time, and into Decompositional time, where only chemicals battle with each other for existence. You will see that Silverstone comes from the last days of the world."

And back came Howes' tiny reflection, soft and enduring as a grain of pollen: "Then we shall die..."

They were standing they scarcely knew where, after experiencing they scarcely knew what.

At once Howes, and then Borrow, Ann, and Bush, clutched at their throats; no oxygen was seeping through their air-leakers. They were so many geochrons back towards the end – the beginning – of the world, that the gases on which human life depended were now locked away in the groaning interior of the globe in non-volatile combinations.

"You are safe!" Wygelia cried, pointing at the four pall-bearers. Each had erected hollow rods like aerials from the cases on their backs; these rods now fumed fiercely like half-lit torches of tar. "We have our own means of supplying oxygen and nitrogen in these barren places," she said. "We are further protected from the conditions outside by a sphere of force operating within the entropy barrier, so we are free from all harm here."

As she reassured them, they could draw the air into their lungs and take time to view their surroundings.

The earth, sinking towards its end, was in a semi-molten state. The temperature beyond their protective sphere and beyond the entropy wall was several thousand degrees centigrade. It seemed to be the hour of dawn, but there had surely been no proper night on this deliquescing planet. All about them was a sea of ash, patched with streaks of broken light which radiated upwards. The sea heaved; the ash was but a thin crust, covering an unending gleet of molten rock.

Their little party, with the body of Silverstone central among them, stood on the generalized floor of mind-travel which roughly coincided with the surface of an enormous slab of rock perhaps half a mile wide. Like the sea, the rock had a slow uneasy motion; it floated like an iceberg on the magma; like an iceberg, it would dissolve and be gone.

Bush stared at the scene. No awe took him. He felt nothing. For the time being, he filed away Wygelia's information that he would marry – had married Ann; by some trick of mentality, all he could recall now was little Joan Bush marrying, for obscure reasons, the man who managed what had once been her father's grocery shop. The image of her, the loving arm about her father, was close to him, perhaps prompted by this new revelation of a familiar relationship. Something that had no closer name than longing rose in him; he could scarcely see that her life was any less important than earth's.

Turning to Wygelia, interrupting quite unconsciously her conversation with Ann, he said, "You followed me to many places. You knew the miners' village and Joan; you saw what happened to Herbert."

She nodded. "You began to find your real self there – or by my terms you lost yourself."

"Am I right? By your terms, what happened in Breedale was less of a tragedy than by mine."

"In what respect?"

"You saw Herbert's end. Things grew more and more impossible for him. In the end, he could see only to cut his throat and run bleeding to die in the garden. His wife's end was as wretched. Joan – I believe she married for money rather than for love, which would be bound to bring her nothing but sorrow.

That story could be multiplied thousands of times just in her generation, couldn't it?

"Now, look at it all as it really was, without the occulting lens of the overmind! Joan would emerge from the loveless marriage and come home one day to find her father quiet in the weeds, soon to be born. Her mother would similarly come to life and her miserable pregnancy terminate in time. The man would arrive and return her little shop to her. They would all grow younger. The mine would work again, everyone would be employed. Gradually, the family would grow smaller, burdens light, hope greater. Joan, we presume, would sink into a happy babyhood and finally be taken into her mother, who would grow young and fair again. There'd be no tragedy and very much less distress.

"I realize now why that period I spent minding in Breedale was so vital to me. I saw how most human sin is the result of most human misery; it was misery and above all the misery of *uncertainty* that made me do the base acts in my life. Once rid of the overmind, you – everyone – can suffer no uncertainty, because you know the future. What happened to Joan, a loving creature who in the end denied love, is like a history of everyone under overmind.

"So tell me, what terrible affliction brought down the overmind on humanity? What happened on the Himalayas?"

Borrow said quietly, "I don't know what this particular experience of yours with Joan was, Eddie, but that was the question I was going to ask Silverstone – and Wygelia. Why all this, in heaven's name, from the Stone Age men to us?"

"You deserve an answer, and I will give it to you as simply as possible, trying to relate it in your terms," Wygelia said. She looked down at the composed face of Norman Silverstone on his bier before continuing, as if to gather strength.

"Nothing has yet been said to you of the long past of the human race – the future as you learnt to see it. But you must know that that past has been extremely long – a dozen

Cryptozoics placed on end, covering untold epochs. The growth of the overmind was a rapid thing, spread over only two or three generations.

"The overmind grew from the first serious mental disturbance we had ever known – for we never had the history of tragedy and mental suffering and pain that you did, on your side of the Himalayas. That disturbance was brought about by the realization that the end of earth was drawing near. You cannot imagine the powers or the glories of our race; for though you are children of ours and we children of yours, and there is no break in the succession, yet we existed under different natural laws from you, as Silverstone explained, and created with them – well, many things you would find too miraculous to be credible, mind-travel on a formidable scale being but one of them. We were almost a perfect race – you would say 'will be'.

"Can you imagine the bitterness such a people would experience to realize that in their great days the planet they lived on would die, and the system of which it was a part? *We* were not hardened as you to numberless sorrows, we did not know sorrow, and a mass-sickness – a revulsion from time that dragged us to the brink of the catastrophe – overtook us all.

"We think it was an evolutionary sickness. Our next generation, or in some cases the next generation but one, was born (died, as you would say) with the upper part of the mind reversed in temporal polarity, so that they perceive as you perceive, because they are you.

"And we can see now that this reversal is the greatest mercy, that – "

"Wait, Wygelia!" Bush said. "*How* can you call it a mercy when you admit that if we – if the people at Breedale – could see their lives right way round they would be happier? And so back through recorded history, through all the ancient civilizations!"

She answered him firmly, without hesitation. "I call it merciful because you have had the distraction of all your smaller pains to hide the larger pain from you."

"You can't say that! Think of Herbert Bush bursting into the garden with his throat choking blood! What more pain than that?"

"Why, the pain of being fully aware of your glorious faculties slipping away one by one, generation by generation. Of seeing the engineers constructing ever cruder engines; the governments losing their enlightenment in favour of slavery; the builders pulling down comfortable houses, building less convenient ones; the chemists degenerating into old men looking for a metal to transmute into gold; the surgeons abandoning their elaborate equipment to take up hacksaws; the citizens forgetting their scruples to run to a public hanging – this all happens only a pathetic few generations after you four fade back into your mothers. Could you bear that? It's the senescence of an entire species! Could you bear to see the last rudiments of agriculture lost before a grubby nomadism? Could you bear to see huts exchanged for poor caves? Could you bear to see human eye grow dull as intelligence left it?

"And then everything else begins to senesce, even the plants, even the reptiles and amphibians. With mind-travel, you have been able to see them climb out on to the land and populate it. However cynical you were, you must have taken hope and reassurance from it! But suppose you saw that process through our clear eyes. Would you not love the lumbering Permian amphibians, however crude, however incomplete, as tokens of the grandeur that had once been on earth? And when those amphibians lumbered backwards into the mud and swamp and dwindled into finny things, would you not weep? Would you not weep when the last green pseudo-seaweed slipped back off the rocks into the warm sea for the last time? When the trilobites vanished? When life died into mud?

"That terrible process, the senescence of earth, could never be reversed! Mankind has to go the hard way into the scuttling mindless world of the jungle, the jungle on the ineluctable tide of time has to shrink back into seaweeds, and all that was dissolved into the fire and ash we see about us. No escape – no hope of escape! But the overmind fell like a vizor and protected mankind from realizing the full horror of his ultimate decay."

chapter nine

god of galaxies

They buried Silverstone then: or, as they had begun to see it should be, they received his body from nature – and this mucilaginous world of flowing rock was the wildest face of nature any of them would ever gaze upon.

The force sphere was manipulated by Wygelia. The bier bearing the professor's body was set down and the sphere then distorted, so that the bier was borne into a long extension of it; the extension closed in on itself and broke off, in a manner reminiscent of a bubble of glass being blown. With the body inside it, this bubble drifted down from the mass of floating rock. It hovered over the ocean of heaving ash and then touched it. At once, a great jet, a block of liquid flame, rose high into the heavy air. The bubble flashed and disappeared. It was all over except for a great line of light that split across the glutinous waste and disappeared.

In a moved voice, Howes said, "We should have had a bugle. We should have sounded 'Last Post'."

" 'Reveille'," Borrow corrected him.

There seemed nothing more to say. They stood gazing out over the fantastic scene. It was full day now. A strong wind was moving, calling sparks from the waste; a few more millennia and all would be fire; their island would melt like a candle in a furnace. The wind was breaking up the cloud, which had lain across the entire sky like slate strata and seemingly as solid. The strata tore away in mighty patches more reminiscent of islands than clouds, and revealed the sun.

The sun blazed; yet it was dark and blotched. It trailed streamers of fire. It was an augur of the final inferno to come.

"Well, we'll be getting back to 2093 now, Wygelia," Howes said, forcing a conversational officer's voice. "Just one thing I'd like to ask before we go. We're going back to trouble. How do I – er, meet my – birth?"

"You meet it triumphantly, Captain. Bravely and far from uselessly. That's all you should know. And you fully understand now?"

"Haven't any option, have I? And I know what I'm going to do when we return, what my strategy will be. I shall report to my own revolutionary force first, of course. Then I shall give myself up to the Action Party. They'll take me before Gleason. And I'll tell him – all this, about the overmind."

"Will you convert him?" Borrow asked.

"I'll see that I shake him. Or, given the chance, I'll kill him."

"I suppose after all this we'd better get in some action too," Ann said. "I won't know how to start explaining, though."

"Here's a bit of proof nobody has mentioned so far," Bush said. "Perhaps I take it from my own life, perhaps from Breedale – more likely from everywhere. You and I talked about incest, Ann. That's the point where the join between overmind and undermind is weakest – naturally, because it is the point where life and death, birth and death, become confused. The ban against the incest – we said no animal allows such a ban; it was invented to stop us looking back to our parents, because the undermind knew all along that that way was death, not life. In the past, you don't have any ban against incest, do you, Wygelia?"

She shook her dark head. "No. Nor do we have incest, since we all return anyway to our parents."

Howes shook his head. "I think I'll stick to gunpoint for my conversations."

"I'm not a soldier," Borrow said firmly. "But I will certainly be happy to do what Silverstone charged me with. Give me a chance to collect Ver from the Amniote Egg and I will begin interpretive montages straight away. I can explain the situation in arty circles – they'll soon disseminate it."

"Are you coming with us to 2093?" Bush asked Wygelia.

She shook her dark head, smiling sadly.

"I have done all Central Authority asked of me. My mission is done and I am not permitted to do more. But I shall see you and Ann again when I am a child. Before I leave you, the four men here and I will accompany you in mind-travel to the threshold of 2093."

They were mind-travelling again, drawing back from the end of the world that they had long regarded as the beginning.

Both Ann and Bush floated a question to Wygelia together.

Bush, a million spirals, mainly mauve rattling: "If – the long past of the race – humanity – was so great, why remain on this one planet to die? Why not escape to other worlds?"

Ann, interlocking yellow circles: "Tell us – give us just a glimpse of that great past."

Wygelia warned them she would answer both questions at once.

She released a great white castle. It floated at them and through, being transformed by their minds' touch as it went, and crossed a dizzying space. It had many rooms. Its walls interlocked and interpenetrated. It was an elaborate structuring of universe-history, a popularization which they might vaguely comprehend, formulated by a mastermind. It was also the supreme artwork. This, Bush and Borrow would spend the rest of their lives searching for, forgetting, trying to recreate, handing something of the paradoxical glory of it down to other artists such as Picasso and Turner.

Some of its meaning they grasped, as they swam like fish through its elucidations.

Long past, immeasurably long past, the human race had been born into creation at a myriad points at once. It was as diffuse as gas. It was pure intellect. It was omnipotent.

It was God.

It had been God and it had created the universe. It had then been governed by its own laws. In the course of untold eons it entered more fully into its own creation. It had become planet-bound and occupied many millions of planets. Gradually, over countless forgotten eons, it had drawn in upon itself, like a large family returning to the same roof in the afternoon, when work is done. To grow together had meant the shedding of abilities; that had not mattered. Other abilities remained. Soon the planets became drained of human life, whole galaxies were evacuated. But the galaxies were themselves gathering together, rushing closer.

The long long process... Nothing now left in the race expressed it. Finally, all that remained of the shining multitude was congregated on earth. The great symphony of creation was reached, a conclusion long since arranged.

"It's a consolation – we have legends of the truth in our religions," Bush thought.

"Memories!" Wygelia corrected. From the tenor of her thoughts they took consolation for their fallen state.

The great castle had permeated them for longer than they had suspected. She was guiding them in to surface, she would set them miraculously in a safe place, close to one of the anti-Action strongholds.

They surfaced. Wygelia had gone, the four pall-bearers had gone, Howes was already looking alert and ready for action. Ann and Bush turned and looked at each other, softly, yet challengingly.

"You've still damned well got to persuade me!" she said.

"I'll persuade you," Bush said. "But first I'm going to find Wenlock and give him the word."

"Good idea," Howes said. "Come with me to the rebel hideout – they'll give you the name of the mental institution where Wenlock's being held."

Turning they followed him through the ruins of their own trans-Himalayan age.

A nurse was walking along the grey corridor. James Bush, LDS, jerked his head up and came fully awake. Looking at his watch, he saw that he had been sitting waiting on the uncomfortable metal seat for twenty minutes.

The nurse came up to him and said, "The Supervisor is still engaged, Mr Bush. The Deputy Supervisor, Mr Frankland, will see you, if you will follow me."

She turned about and marched off in the direction she had come, so that the dentist had to rise hastily and follow. At the far end of the corridor, they climbed a flight of stairs, and the nurse showed him through a door on which the name ALBERT FRANKLAND was painted.

A plump untidy man with rimless spectacles and a fussy manner rose from behind his desk and came forward to offer James a chair.

"I'm Mr Frankland, the Deputy Supervisor of Carlfield Advanced Mental Disturbances Institution, Mr Bush. We're very pleased to see you here, and of course if there is anything we can do to help, you have only to ask."

The words released the sense of grievance that had been building up in James. "I want to see my son! That's all! It's simple enough, isn't it? Yet this is the fourth time I've come here in two weeks, only to be sent away each time without any satisfaction! It costs money, you know, getting up here, and the travelling isn't easy nowadays."

Frankland was beaming and nodding and tapping a finger approvingly on the desk edge, as if he understood exactly what

James was getting at. "You're implying an oblique criticism of the Party when you condemn public transport like that, I expect," he said conspiratorially.

His smile, from the other side of the desk, suddenly looked ugly. James drew back. More calmly, he said, "I'm asking to see my son Ted, that's all."

Looking hard at him. Frankland bit his lower lip. Finally, he said. "You know your son's suffering from a dangerous delusory madness, don't you?"

"I don't know anything. I can't learn anything! Why can't I even see him?"

Frankland started picking his nails, looked down to see what his hands were doing, and then shot a glance at James under his brows. "To tell you the truth, he's under sedation. That's why you can't see him. The last time you came to this Institution, he had escaped from his cell on the previous day and ran about the corridors causing quite a bit of damage and attacking a female nurse and a male orderly. In his delusory state, he believed he was in Buckingham Palace."

"Buckingham Palace!"

"Buckingham Palace. What do you make of that? Too much mind-travel, that's the basic trouble, coming on top of, er – hereditary weaknesses. He spent too long in mind-travel. Of course, we're still in the early days of mind-travel, but we are beginning to understand that the peculiar anosmic conditions pertaining to it can help to fragment the mind. Anosmic, meaning without sense of smell – the olfactory centres of the brain are the most ancient ones. Your son started to believe he could mind into human-habited ages, and a long series of delusions followed which we are hoping to record and study, to help with future cases."

"Look, Mr Frankland, I don't want to hear about future cases – I just want to hear about Ted! You say mind-travel upset him? He seemed all right to me when he came home after being two-and-a-half years away, after his mother died."

"We aren't always good judges of another's mental health, Mr Bush. Your son at that time was ready to be pushed into madness by any sudden shock. He was already suffering from an aggravated form of anomia."

"No sense of smell?"

"That's anosmia, Mr Bush. I'm speaking now of a far more serious state, anomia. It looks like being the great mental disease that is going to dog mind-travellers. An anomic individual is quite isolated; he feels cut off from society and all its broad social values; he becomes normless and disgusted with life as it is. In mind-travel, seeing a world about him he is powerless to influence in any way, the anomic individual thinks of life as being without goal or meaning. He tends to turn back into his own past, to turn back the clock, to regress into a catatonic womb-state."

"You're blinding me by science, Mr Frankland," said James, aggrievedly. "As I say, Ted seemed okay when he came home that time."

"And the outside world conspired to give your son that requisite extra push," Frankland continued, nodding slightly to James as an indication that he reckoned it kinder to ignore his interruption. "That push, of course, was the death of his mother. We know he had an incestuous fixation for her, and the discovery that she had finally eluded his desires sent your son off on a startling manic trajectory that was a masked attempt to turn back to the womb."

"It doesn't sound like Ted at all."

Frankland rose. "Since you don't seem disposed to believe me, I will give you a little proof."

He walked over to a portable tape recorder, selected a tape from a nearby rack, set it on the spindle, and switched on.

"We have recorded a great deal of what your son has said in his hallucinatory periods. Here's a fragment from very early in his treatment, when he was first brought here. I should explain that he collapsed while waiting to be interviewed by

Mr Howells, his superior at the Wenlock Institute. For reasons we do not yet understand, he was convinced that our great Head of State, General Peregrine Bolt, was imposing an evil régime on the country. This sort of case always regards itself as persecuted. Later, in his mind, he supplanted General Bolt by a figure he could more satisfactorily regard as evil, an Admiral Gleason; but at the time of his recording, he was not too deeply sunk in his delusions. At least he still believed himself to be in this age, and had some sort of conversation with his doctor and some students, as you'll hear."

He switched the recorder on. Muffled noises, a groan. An indistinct mutter, resolving itself into a name: Howes. A precise voice, neutral in tone, commenting, "The patient when reporting to the institute believed his superior, Howells, to be a man named Franklin. Franklin is a distortion of my name, Frankland; the patient was brought before me when he collapsed. The name Howells occurs, again slightly distorted, as one of the participants – a captain – in the patient's military imaginings. Your son was caught in a distorted subjective world when we recorded this."

The muttering voice on the tape came suddenly to clarity and was recognizable as Eddie Bush's; he asked, "I'm not dying, am I?"

It sounded as if there were several students about him, talking to each other in low tones.

"He can't understand a thing you say."

"He's tuned only to his own needs."

"He imagines himself in another place, perhaps another time."

"Hasn't he committed incest?"

Again came Bush's voice, now very loud: "Where do you fellows think I am?"

And again the other voices, mainly admonitory.

"Quietly!"

"You'll wake the others in the ward up."

"You're suffering from anomia, with auditory hallu-cinations."

"But the window's open," Bush replied, as if the mysterious remark explained everything "Where is this, anyway?"

"You're in Carlfield Mental Hospital."

"We're looking after you."

"We believe you are an anomia case."

"Your meeting's scrambled," Bush said.

Frankland switched off the recorder, pursing his lips, shaking his head.

"Very sad case, Mr Bush. At the time of that recording, your son believed himself to be in some kind of a barrack-room; he was unable to accept that he was in a hospital ward. From that time on, he retreated further and further from reality into his own imaginings. At one point, he became violent and attacked a specialist with a metal crutch. We had to place him in isolation for a while, in the new Motherbeer Wing here – "

James broke in on the recital, crying, "Ted's all I have! Of course, he was never a religious boy, but he was a good boy! He'd never meant to be violent... Never..."

"You have my sympathies. Of course, we are doing what we can for him..."

"Poor old Ted! At least you can let me see him!"

"That would not be advisable. He believes you to be dead."

"Dead!"

"Yes, dead. He believes he entered into a deal with army authorities who agreed to supply you with drink, significantly called Black Wombat, with which you drank yourself to death. Your son thus managed – mentally, of course – to murder you and lay the guilt at someone else's door."

James shook his head, almost in imitation of Frankland. "Anomia...I don't understand at all, I really don't. Such a quiet boy, a good artist..."

"Yes, they're always the type who go, I'm afraid," Frankland said, looking at his wristwatch. "To tell you the truth, we hope art therapy may aid him a little. Art enters into his hallucinatory states. So do most strands of his life. I would not agree with you that your son is not religious. One aspect of his case presents itself as what the layman would probably term religious mania. You see, the search for perfection, for an end to unhappiness, is very strong in him. At one time – this was when he was in solitary confinement – I mean, in Motherbeer – he attempted to construct an ideal family unit in which he could find peace. We have the tapes of that period in his illness; they are very harrowing. In that hypothetical family unit, your son plays the father role, thus symbolically usurping your part. The father was, significantly an out-of-work miner. Members of the nursing staff were pressed into other roles of his fantasy."

"What happened?"

"Your son was unable to sustain the illusion of peace for long; the pressure was on him to slip back to a state of more open terror, to a paradigm of hunters and hunted, kill or be killed. So the family unit construct was brutally dissolved in self-hate: he ended with a symbolic suicide, which heralded a complete abdication of reason and a return to the womb-state which is the ultimate goal of incest-fixated natures. He ceased to relate. You invited these details, Mr Bush."

"Ceased to relate... But it doesn't sound like my boy. Of course, I know he was involved with women..."

Frankland permitted himself a short growl of laughter.

" 'Involved with women'! Yes. Your son, Mr Bush – your son knows only one woman, his mother, and all other females he meets are identified with her. Hence, he never seeks or finds permanence with any of them, for fear they might dominate him.

"His obsessive-compulsive tendencies have collapsed into schizophrenia oriented about this psychic disturbance. He experiences his anima – his *anima*, or female actuating spirit, not to be confused with anomia or anosmia – as detached from

himself, as a separate entity. This entity he called his Dark
Woman. She originally fulfilled the classic function of animae by
watching over him."

"Dark Woman? Never heard of her!"

"Now, in the later stages of your son's illness, the Dark
Woman becomes transformed into yet another replication of
the incest-figure, a female at once mother and daughter, this
signifying the accelerating mental deterioration of the subject."

James Bush looked about the hateful room without
particularly wishing to see it. The chilly words, which he did not
fully understand or fully believe, drove hint back into himself.
He needed escape as much as he needed to see Ted; and of
escapes, he could not say which he most needed, a good long
prayer session or a good deep drink. Frankland's voice droned
on, not always without a certain relish in its tone.

"On his last mind into the Devonian, when this tragic illness
was brewing, he had intercourse with a young woman called
Ann. She also became involved in your son's fantasies. That
wasn't too successful, either. He believes she is now watching
this institution, and will soon lead an attempt to rescue him.
Significantly, he pictures her as a scruffy dirty underdeveloped
girl. 'Lank-haired whore!' he called her once. Very significantly,
he killed her off at one point and then resurrected her. Very
tragic, a brilliant mind! 'What a brilliant mind is here
o'erthrown!' as the poet has it. But I really mustn't take up any
more of your time…" He rose, and inclined his head.

"Mr Frankland, you've been very kind," James said
desperately. "Let me just have a peep at the poor lad. He's all I
have, you know!"

"Oh, indeed!" Frankland looked surprised and lent forward
over the desk, putting his conspiratorial air again. "I
understood you had connexions with a Mrs Annivale, a widow."

"Well, yes, I – there is a lady of that name lives next door
to me."

Somewhat excessive nodding. "The mind plays strange tricks with names. And, of course, there are strange coincidences to be accounted for. Ann, Annivale, anomia... Do you know what an amnion is?"

"No. Can't I just *peep* in?"

"He'd be upset if he saw you. I told you, now, Mr Bush, he believes you to be dead."

"How could he see me if he was under sedation?"

"He is working on his latest groupage. We give him materials to keep him quiet. It absorbs all his time, but he might turn and notice you and become upset."

"You said he was under sedation."

"No, no, that was yesterday. I said he was under sedation yesterday. And now Mr Bush, really..."

James could see the interview was at an end. He made one last desperate effort. "Why don't you let me take him away from here? I'll look after him – he won't come to any harm! I mean – what are you *doing* for him here? What hope is there of a cure?"

Looking extremely grave, Frankland prodded the top button of James' mackintosh with an extended finger and said, "You laymen always underestimate the gravity of extreme mental illness. Sometimes the mind seems to be thrown into civil war. Your son believes that time is flowing backwards! He does not believe in your universe any more, Mr Bush, and he needs official restraint. To tell you the truth, a cure is hardly to be hoped for at present. Our duty is to keep him quiet. Now, I'll see you as far as the hall, if I may."

He was nudging James to the door, opening it. In the corridor, a scuffle was going on. A lean man clad in grey pyjamas stood in a doorway a little way off, struggling to get away from two female nurses. He was calling for the supervisor.

"Doctor Wenlock, you must come back to bed!" one of the nurses said, tugging at his arm.

"Excuse me!" Frankland exclaimed, and ran down the corridor towards the struggling group. Before he got there, a burly orderly in a white overall emerged from inside the room, put a hand over the patient's face, and dragged him ruthlessly back out of sight. The door slammed. The incident was over in a few seconds.

Frankland returned, red in the face. "I have other work to do, Mr Bush – work of a rather pressing nature. No doubt you can find your own way out."

There was nothing for it but to go.

The Carlfield Institution stood in ample grounds, bounded by a high wall. The dentist knew he could catch a bus fairly close to the front gates. With only two changes of bus, he could be home, but the connexions were bad and few buses ran. It was raining steadily.

He had no hat. He wound his scarf over his head and pulled up the collar of his thin mack before setting off bravely down the drive. It would be good to get home and have a drink.

Frankland had defeated him, of course. Next time he came, he would demand to see one of Ted's groupages that he was supposed to be working on. It was all very distressing.

Ceased to relate, indeed! He and Ted would always be related, whatever happened to the boy. Of course, the blame for this could partly be laid at Lavinia's door; no, that wasn't fair; it was to do with the time they were living in. James began to pray as the rain whipped him.

The drive was a long one. He could feel his legs getting wet through his trousers. He'd have to have a mustard bath when he got home, if there was enough mustard left, otherwise he'd be laid up. What misery it was, growing old, and at times like these! O Lord, in thy infinite mercy look down…

They checked his pass at the gate and he walked through into the undistinguished street. Head down as he moved towards the bus stop, he never noticed the slight-figured girl standing watching under a tree, water dripping from her lank fair hair. She could have touched him as he passed.

O Lord, in thy infinite mercy…

BRIAN ALDISS

THE AIRS OF EARTH

This classic collection of stories contains eight excursions into the imagination and poetry of Aldiss' writing. It poses such questions as how the human mind would respond in a non-human body, and whether universal laughter, secreted from a kidney, could save the world.

Among the treasures: On a remote planet, the great Cliff that learns to understand life; segregated life forms demanding sexual release; one hundred and fifty thousand dead after an H-bomb drops in World War II, while Britain remains neutral; and the old baluchitherium woman trundling towards release on an Earth transformed.

BAREFOOT IN THE HEAD

When an undeclared Acid Head War breaks out, Britain is the first to be devastated by Psycho-Chemical Aerosols – tasteless, odourless, colourless psychedelic drugs, which distort the minds of thousands of civilians into extreme terror or extreme joy. When the warped citizens of Europe proclaim Colin Charteris their hero, he finds himself leading an unfathomable crusade in a devastated world.

Barefoot in the Head has long been regarded as a psychedelic triumph of a novel.

BRIAN ALDISS

DRACULA UNBOUND

Supernatural horror merges with science fiction in this extraordinary quest beyond life, death and time.

While Bram Stoker is writing his famous novel, *Dracula*, at the end of the nineteenth century, he receives a visitor from the future, Joe Bodenland, who is on a desperate mission to save the human race from the Undead. Together they embark on a crusade to exterminate vampires – a trail which begins in twenty-first century Utah and ends up far away in space and time, in a devastating climax that changes the world forever.

FRANKENSTEIN UNBOUND

This stunning blend of horror, excitement, suspense and love takes place when a timeslip enables Joe Bodenland to visit a past containing not only Byron, Shelley and Mary Shelley – her great book half-written – but Frankenstein and his monster as well. The climax is played out against the frozen wastes of time.

Kingsley Amis said of this novel, 'The mating dance of the two monsters has a macabre beauty quite new to me'.

Roger Corman filmed *Frankenstein Unbound*. The film starred John Hurt and Bridget Fonda.

Brian Aldiss

Hothouse

The Sun is about to go nova. Earth and Moon have ceased their axial rotation and present one face continuously to the Sun. The bright side of Earth is covered with carnivorous forest.

This is the Age of Vegetables. Gren and his lady – not to mention the tummybelly men – journey to the even more terrifying Dark Side. One of Aldiss' most famous and long-enduring novels, fast moving, packed with brilliant imagery.

Moreau's Other Island

Under-Secretary of State, Calvert Roberts, is washed up on Moreau Island, ruled over by the bionic Mortimer Dart. Dart is experimenting with genetic modification on a grand scale.

The doomed inhabitants of the island endure a precarious balance between human and animal nature. The result is a horrific adventure not unmixed with comedy.

The human future is being reprogrammed. A shock awaits Roberts when he discovers who is responsible for the nightmare.

OTHER TITLES BY BRIAN ALDISS AVAILABLE DIRECT
FROM HOUSE OF STRATUS

Quantity	£	$(US)	$(CAN)	€
THE AIRS OF EARTH	6.99	11.50	15.99	11.50
BAREFOOT IN THE HEAD	6.99	11.50	15.99	11.50
DRACULA UNBOUND	6.99	11.50	15.99	11.50
FRANKENSTEIN UNBOUND	6.99	11.50	15.99	11.50
HOTHOUSE	6.99	11.50	15.99	11.50
MOREAU'S OTHER ISLAND	6.99	11.50	15.99	11.50
THE MOMENT OF ECLIPSE	6.99	11.50	15.99	11.50

COMING SOON

	£	$(US)	$(CAN)	€
THE BRIGHTFOUNT DIARIES	6.99	11.50	15.99	11.50
BURY MY HEART AT W H SMITH'S	6.99	11.50	15.99	11.50
THE MALACIA TAPESTRY	6.99	11.50	15.99	11.50
MAN IN HIS TIME	6.99	11.50	15.99	11.50
THE PRIMAL URGE	6.99	11.50	15.99	11.50
A RUDE AWAKENING	6.99	11.50	15.99	11.50
A SOLDIER ERECT	6.99	11.50	15.99	11.50
TRILLION YEAR SPREE: THE HISTORY OF SCIENCE FICTION	6.99	11.50	15.99	11.50

ALL HOUSE OF STRATUS BOOKS ARE AVAILABLE FROM GOOD BOOKSHOPS
OR DIRECT FROM THE PUBLISHER:

Internet: www.houseofstratus.com including author interviews, reviews, features.

Email: sales@houseofstratus.com please quote author, title and credit card details.

OTHER TITLES BY BRIAN ALDISS AVAILABLE DIRECT
FROM HOUSE OF STRATUS

Quantity		£	$(US)	$(CAN)	€
	BROTHERS OF THE HEAD	6.99	11.50	15.99	11.50
	THE DARK LIGHT YEARS	6.99	11.50	15.99	11.50
	EARTHWORKS	6.99	11.50	15.99	11.50
	THE EIGHTY-MINUTE HOUR: A SPACE OPERA	6.99	11.50	15.99	11.50
	ENEMIES OF THE SYSTEM	6.99	11.50	15.99	11.50
	EQUATOR	6.99	11.50	15.99	11.50
	GALAXIES LIKE GRAINS OF SAND	6.99	11.50	15.99	11.50
	GREYBEARD	6.99	11.50	15.99	11.50
	INTANGIBLES INC. AND OTHER STORIES	6.99	11.50	15.99	11.50
	LAST ORDERS AND OTHER STORIES	6.99	11.50	15.99	11.50
	THE MALE RESPONSE	6.99	11.50	15.99	11.50
	NEW ARRIVALS, OLD ENCOUNTERS	6.99	11.50	15.99	11.50
	REPORT ON PROBABILITY A	6.99	11.50	15.99	11.50
	A ROMANCE OF THE EQUATOR	6.99	11.50	15.99	11.50
	THE SALIVA TREE	6.99	11.50	15.99	11.50
	SEASONS IN FLIGHT	6.99	11.50	15.99	11.50
	THE SHAPE OF FURTHER THINGS	6.99	11.50	15.99	11.50
	SPACE, TIME AND NATHANIEL	6.99	11.50	15.99	11.50

ALL HOUSE OF STRATUS BOOKS ARE AVAILABLE FROM GOOD BOOKSHOPS
OR DIRECT FROM THE PUBLISHER:

Hotline: UK ONLY: 0800 169 1780, please quote author, title and credit card details.
INTERNATIONAL: +44 (0) 20 7494 6400, please quote author, title, and credit card details.

Send to: **House of Stratus**
24c Old Burlington Street
London
W1X 1RL
UK

Please allow following carriage costs per ORDER
(For goods up to free carriage limits shown)

	£(Sterling)	$(US)	$(CAN)	€(Euros)
UK	1.95	3.20	4.29	3.00
Europe	2.95	4.99	6.49	5.00
North America	2.95	4.99	6.49	5.00
Rest of World	2.95	5.99	7.75	6.00
Free carriage for goods value over:	50	75	100	75

PLEASE SEND CHEQUE, POSTAL ORDER (STERLING ONLY), EUROCHEQUE, OR INTERNATIONAL MONEY ORDER (PLEASE CIRCLE METHOD OF PAYMENT YOU WISH TO USE) MAKE PAYABLE TO: STRATUS HOLDINGS plc

Order total including postage:_____Please tick currency you wish to use and add total amount of order:

☐ £ (Sterling)   ☐ $ (US)   ☐ $ (CAN)   ☐ € (EUROS)

VISA, MASTERCARD, SWITCH, AMEX, SOLO, JCB:

☐☐☐☐☐☐☐☐☐☐☐☐☐☐☐☐☐☐☐☐☐☐

Issue number (Switch only):

☐☐☐

Start Date: **Expiry Date:**

☐☐/☐☐   ☐☐/☐☐

Signature: _____

NAME: _____

ADDRESS: _____

_____

POSTCODE: _____

Please allow 28 days for delivery.

Prices subject to change without notice.
Please tick box if you do not wish to receive any additional information. ☐

House of Stratus publishes many other titles in this genre; please check our website (**www.houseofstratus.com**) for more details